Richard Dee is a native of Brixham in Devon. He left Devon when he was in his teens and settled in Kent. Leaving school at 16 he briefly worked in a supermarket, then went to sea and travelled the world in the Merchant Navy, qualifying as a Master Mariner in 1986.

Coming ashore to be with his growing family, he used his sea-going knowledge in several jobs, working as a Marine Insurance Surveyor and as Dockmaster at Tilbury, before becoming a Port Control Officer in Sheerness and then at the Thames Barrier in Woolwich.

In 1994 he was head-hunted and offered a job as a Thames Estuary Pilot. In 1999 he transferred to the Thames River Pilots, where he regularly took vessels of all sizes through the Thames Barrier and upriver as far as HMS *Belfast* and through Tower Bridge. In all, he piloted over 3,500 vessels in a 22-year career with the Port of London Authority.

Richard is married with three adult children and two grandchildren.

His first science-fiction novel *Freefall* was published in 2013, followed by *Ribbonworld* in 2015. September 2016 saw the publication of his Steampunk adventure *The Rocks of Aserol* and of *Flash Fiction*, a collection of Short Stories. *Myra*, the prequel to *Freefall* was published in 2017, along with *Andorra Pett and the Oort Cloud Café*, a murder mystery set in space and the start of a series featuring Andorra Pett, an amateur detective. He contributed a story to the *1066 Turned Upside Down* collection and is currently working on prequels, sequels, and new projects.

He can be found at www.richarddeescifi.co.uk and contacted at richarddeescifi@gmail.com

Also by Richard Dee

The Dave Travise Series
Freefall
Myra

The Balcom Series
Ribbonworld
Jungle Green

Steampunk
The Rocks of Aserol
A New Life in Ventis
Tales from Norlandia

Andorra Pett
Andorra Pett and the Oort Cloud Café

Short Stories
Flash Fiction

Andorra Pett On Mars

Richard Dee

All rights reserved.

ISBN 978-0-9954581-9-2 (Paperback)

978-1-9996376-0-6 (eBook)

Published in 2018 by 4Star Scifi

4Star Scifi, Brixham, Devon, England

www.richarddeescifi.co.uk/4Star

Copyright © Richard Dee 2017

No part of this publication may be reproduced, stored in a retrieval system, or transmitted in any form or by any means, electronic, mechanical, photocopying, recording, or otherwise, without the prior written permission of the copyright owner.

This book is sold subject to the condition that it shall not, by way of trade or otherwise, be lent, resold, hired out, or otherwise circulated without the publisher's prior consent in any form of binding or cover other than that in which it is published and without a similar condition including this condition being imposed on the subsequent purchaser. Under no circumstances may any part of this book be photocopied for resale.

This is a work of fiction. Any similarity between the characters and situations within its pages and places or persons, living or dead, is unintentional and coincidental.

Cover by Avalon Graphics.

For the original four stars,
not forgetting the new arrivals

Chapter 1

What was I doing here? Not for the first time I wondered that as I faced the man who had changed my life in so many ways. He had cheated on me and I was now pretty sure that he had been responsible for the death of my oldest friend. For what? The usual of course, money! Oh, and to try and save his own miserable neck.

The gun was pointed at me, this was it, where was my backup? I was in urgent need of a knight on a white charger; Mayner and his merry men should have turned up by now. Failing that, Cy would do, just as long as he got me out of here pronto! And where the hell had he got to?

In case you hadn't guessed it by now, bloody Trevor had come back into my life in the worst possible way and I hadn't felt able to refuse his sob story. And now here I was back on Mars, a place that I thought I'd left behind. I was only here because Trevor had made me think that I had to help, that to refuse would leave me feeling guilty forever. But as I made sense of things, I realised that I had been deceived. Now it looked like I was going to pay for that misplaced loyalty.

~~~~

Life in the Oort Cloud Café had settled into a pattern once all the excitement had died down and I had exorcised the past. Maz had the book, although she didn't know it, and I had no intention of looking at it. The café was doing well and the atmosphere on the station had improved now that the book had never existed as far as everyone was concerned.

I had done my extra hours training and was now a fully qualified Scooper pilot; I went out every now and again and did a shift to keep my hand in and cover the miners' leave. Cy had even come out with me for a spot of sightseeing. I had started my suit training as well. Tina had talked me into it and after the initial fear it felt very liberating to bob around. I had learned to do a few maintenance tasks on the shuttles and the exterior of the station.

Even better than any of my other achievements, I had finally got off with Derek! We were officially an item, we were happy together and my life was good. I spent a lot of time at his house on the lower farm level and just used the café as a place to work. It was great to wake up to the sound of birds and the smells of the country. There weren't that many people in the solar system who could say that these days.

And then it happened. I might have guessed it, things were all working out, a sure sign that a big boot would come and kick me on the arse.

It was Cy who spotted him; I was in the kitchen chatting with Clarissa. It was pie-making day and I was engaged in a little quality control when he came in looking worried.

"Andi," he said, "don't react but there's someone out there you might not want to see."

I crammed the last of the fruit tart into my mouth and chewed. Then I went to the serving hatch and peered through; my stomach lurched and my head spun. Oh, bloody hell. That was all I needed. Just when I was getting on so well with Derek; a big slice of my past had turned up. The worst thing was that just the sight of him still made me come over all unnecessary. I felt a tingle and my face must have gone red.

"Tell him I'm not here," I said to Cy, "and for goodness' sake get rid of him."

Too late. He walked in; Maz must have told him where I was. Thanks for that!

"Looks like you can tell him yourself," Cy said dryly.

"Hi, Andi." He shuffled about, keeping his distance; wise move. I tried to look him straight in the eye but he was looking anywhere but at me.

"I'm glad to see you," he said, he sounded tired.

"I'll be off then," said Clarissa, sensing the tension that had come into the room with him. She left her stuff on the counter in her haste to leave. Trevor cast an approving eye at her rear as she departed. He hadn't changed that much since I had seen him last then.

It was always either love or hate with me and Trevor; for a long time, it had been hate.

"Go away," I said. "I'm over you, just like you were all over Maisie."

"Ouch! Fair enough. But honestly, I've only come here because I have nowhere else to turn." He had switched on the charm, big eyes and sad face, like a puppy caught next to a puddle.

I didn't believe him, not for a moment. "Why? Has she thrown you out?" I asked as sarcastically as I could. "Caught you at it like I did?"

"It's not that," he whined. "I need your help."

That still didn't cut any ice with me, I was just getting started. "Why should I help you? What about madam fluff doing a bit? Surely she's been very accommodating so far."

"Listen, Andi. I understand I shouldn't be here. I'm a shit and I treated you badly."

That could win a prize for understatement. I was just about to give him some more when I stopped.

His shoulders were shaking and he had started to cry. "Maisie's dead, nearly a fortnight ago," he gasped.

My world stopped turning. I might have fallen out with Maisie when Trevor left me for her but I'd grown up with her, we had history, we'd been friends since our first day in primary school. We'd faced life together and, rather prophetically as it turned out, we had always shared everything. Underneath it all, you couldn't change the memories of the good times. She couldn't be gone. I felt numb and sick at the same time. Beside me, Cy looked like he had been hit by something heavy, his shoulders were slumped and he was welling up. She had been his friend too.

This wasn't happening. "She can't be dead! What's going on, Trevor?" I grabbed him and shook him, then I just held him, burying my head in his shirt front and making it very wet with my tears.

"That's why I need your help," Trevor mumbled into my shoulder. "The police say that it was suicide but I know, I just know that it wasn't."

Bastard! He'd got me in the one place that could still override my desire to rip his bits off, my caring nature. I knew that Maisie would have done it for me. But underneath the grief, I was still on hate. Maisie had been the least likely person to have killed herself, what had changed, apart from the obvious? I pulled away and stood back.

"You'd better tell me all about it then."

"Have you got a spare room, can I stop here?" That was pushing it a bit. The trouble was, despite everything that had happened to extinguish it, the spark was still there. Now that I had seen him, I wondered if I didn't still love him a bit. I dismissed the thought. I was just being stupid. He had betrayed me, now he expected me to forget all that, just cos he wanted something. I had to get a grip! He and I were over; I was happy with Derek. Would I swap? Never.

Looking at him, I realised that he knew exactly what he was doing, his expression and the way he had fed me the story gave it away. Our relationship was all part of my past; I would have to be strong, show him that I didn't need or want him any more.

"No you can't, there's a hostel for visitors, see the admin office." We had a spare room but I wasn't having him too close, I would have to keep him away from Derek until I could explain. How could my life get more complicated?

Cy rolled his eyes and gave a despairing sigh, he could see where this was going, the same as I could, I was getting sucked into Trevor's drama because, in the end, I owed it to my friend more than I did to him.

He was just the bringer of bad tidings. There was always a chance that he might have been responsible, if I found that he had I would take great pleasure in hanging him out to dry. Never mind shoot the messenger, I would do worse than that. And suicide was just so out of character, what had happened in Maisie's life?

"You could have called me before you turned up! I'm not going all the way back to Earth," I said. "I've got a café to run and I'm making a life here."

By leaving it a fortnight he had done me out of going to a funeral and grieving properly. I would have gone too, despite everything.

"Listen, Andi, I know I was stupid and it kills me every day but I really would appreciate your help."

Good, he was grovelling! I thought about it for a while as he squirmed.

"Alright. But never forget, I'm doing it because of her, not for you."

"Thank you," he said, "and you won't have to go back to Earth, this all happened on Mars."

Mars; at least it was neutral territory. "Tell me what happened."

"Maisie went to work like usual. Nobody knows why but she took a vehicle and went outside."

I knew Mars had a city underground in the mountains around Tharsis; a honeycomb of tunnels had been sealed and turned into a city. There were also a few small scientific and prospecting settlements under plastic domes on the outside. I had been to Tharsis with Cy on the way to here. I couldn't say I'd enjoyed it that much, it felt artificial being underground all the time. But that was so close to leaving Earth, now being closed in didn't bother me at all.

"So what were you doing on Mars?"

"We had jobs, I worked in software and she got a job looking after the old people that had settled." That sounded a bit improbable, surely all that money hadn't been spent exploring and colonising the red planet just to turn it into a home for pensioners?

"Mars is an old folks' home?" Cy said what I'd been thinking.

"Oh yeah, they love it, the lower gravity and the sealed environment make them feel ten years younger."

I hadn't thought of that but I guess it made sense.

"Anyhow, I went off to work like usual, then I got a call asking why she hadn't turned up for her shift. I called the police and the next thing I know her vehicle has been found outside, empty; her body was found nearby."

"How did she get outside, did nobody spot her at the airlock?"

"She went out through an old one, unmanned, that's why they reckoned it was suicide, she was found with her suit oxygen tanks empty. She had overdosed on some sort of drug, they said, just driven out, taken the tablets and gone to sleep."

"Did she have any enemies, anyone who might want to hurt her?"

"The police asked me all this, I can't think of anyone but she wasn't unhappy, we were having a great time."

Alright, there was no need to rub it in and tell me how wonderful his life was without me. If it were true, it certainly made the verdict strange; I could sort of understand where Trevor was coming from. But I still didn't want to go, it was too late, I had needed to be there for the funeral.

"Please, Andi; come with me and just have a look around, you'll spot things that I'd miss. And you've got a reputation now. You were all over the news when you caught that murderer."

Now he was appealing to my vanity, I had been rather clever though, it was good to know it had been spotted. Perhaps I could make some outrageous demands that would put him off.

"I'm not coming without Cy and you're paying for the shuttle for us, both ways."

He looked annoyed. "No, just you, I don't want him hanging around." Cy kept his face impassive but I could tell by the way his ears had gone red that old antagonism had been stirred up. It was time to up the ante, see what cards Trevor was holding.

"We both come or you can forget the whole thing," I said, Cy looked at me and shook his head.

It turned out that Trevor wasn't holding any cards; he really must have been desperate.

"OK that's fine, I'll set it all up." This wasn't working, try harder! I turned the knife. "And I want a hotel, a decent one, full board."

"I thought you could stay at mine," he said innocently.

Cy saved my wavering. "Well you thought wrong. If I'm coming I don't want to doss in your place, I want a hotel." Bless him; at least he was still looking out for me, saving me from myself.

Trevor threw his hands up in despair. "Alright, whatever. The shuttle will be leaving tomorrow."

Hang on a minute! That was a bit quick, I hadn't thought he would go for the expense of taking both of us. It wasn't like Trevor to have money to throw around. He must be serious.

"Tomorrow?" I panicked. "I can't just get on a shuttle tomorrow. I have responsibilities, there's one every week, what's the rush?"

"Please, Andi, it's taken me a week to get here, it'll be another one to get back. I had to wait for the investigation to get a verdict, you said you'd come and there's no time to waste."

Put like that it was reasonable but why did I get the feeling that I was being rushed? Surely he could have called me from Mars, or even while he was on the way and we could have talked it over. Trevor had some other agenda; he hadn't mentioned any urgency until I'd agreed to help.

"Pack your bags, I'll go and sort the tickets out. I'll see you at the departure gate in the morning." He rushed out; clearly he had forgotten all about staying in the café. I felt exhausted and numbed by his company and his news. Cy went off muttering. It wasn't just me and Derek, we both had reasons to stay. I finished up the day's work in a bit of a daze.

"Who was that?" asked Maz while we were closing up. "I hope I did right letting him in, he said he knew you and that it was important."

Maz, she was my rock in the café; she had lived on Mars for years, taught school there and knew more about it than I did, I'd only been there a few months, hardly long enough to notice anything about how the place worked. Whatever she could have told me would have been worth it, if only I'd have had the time to ask her.

"That," Cy said grandly, "was Trevor, Andi's ex and the reason we ended up here. And now he's talked her into going off to Mars!" He shook his head. "And I'll have to go and hold her bloody hand, or who knows what'll happen."

Six months ago, he would have been a lot less charitable. Initially he hadn't wanted to be here, never mind want to stay long-term. Events and Greg had persuaded him otherwise.

"He seemed upset." She had spotted that straight off. "Did you say that you're going to Mars?"

"I'm sorry about the short notice, Maz. I need to ask you if you'll manage the café for us. Like Cy says, Trevor needs us to go to Mars for a while. I don't know how long I'll be gone but he needs our help." I wasn't more specific than that. If I tried to explain we would be here all night and I had things to do.

She took it all in her stride, just like the teacher she had been. "Of course I will, I'll tell everyone. Don't you worry about the café; you go and help your friend."

Chapter 2

The shuttle departure lounge wasn't the ideal place to say goodbye. At least Derek and I had managed to do that privately, away from the bright lights and company. I was glad in a way that he hadn't come down here. He said that he had work to do on the farm, but I knew that he really hated public goodbyes. That was OK with me, I hated them too.

We'd spent the evening and night together. I'd come back to the café early to pack and open up. So had Cy, he'd been doing the same with Greg. So when we got to the lounge there were only the two of us, together with the staff and two other passengers. We checked in and then we just stood there, not really believing that we were going. Where was Trevor?

Lou and Terri appeared; they had made the effort to come down from the observatory to see us off and it was sad to be leaving them as well. They were the first people I'd met when we had got here. Together with Tina they had helped me get the café going. They had introduced us to Maz and what a find she had been.

And if it hadn't been for them, I'd never have done half the things I had; no Scooping, no spacewalks and no crime-fighting. I wasn't really sure which bit of my new life I'd enjoyed the most.

Maz had run the café for Mike, the previous owner, and now she was running it for us. Between us we had opened up this morning, then when it was time to go she had seen us off the premises.

"Don't either of you worry, I'll take good care of the place," she had said and I for one knew that she would. "You don't need to rush back, we'll still be here."

Meggie and Claire, my other staff members, were onside with

my trip. "You have to go," they both agreed after I'd told them. "Or you'll never rest."

Lou and Terri both shuffled about and looked sombre. I could have done with them coming with me, they would have been a great help in unravelling Trevor's story. I was convinced that there was more to it than he was letting on.

"We're so sorry about your friend," Lou said as we hugged. They were the only people on the station that knew the full story of Maisie, Trevor and me. As far as everyone else was concerned we had just been a bunch of friends. "It shows real character that you still want to go, after all they put you through."

"It must be horrible, having all those memories stirred up," said Terri. She was right about that. Maisie and I had been besties until the Trevor thing. I wasn't doing this for him though, no matter what he thought. Once I had heard it was suicide, I would have gone even if he had told me not to. It would have made me more determined to find out the truth.

I had had plenty of time to think about what had happened since I had left Earth and I was pretty sure that he had spun her some story to get into her pants. But her dying was different; if someone was responsible then it was important that they were found.

Over time, I had gone through the whole range of emotions. There was the initial feeling of inadequacy that betrayal brought. I hadn't been enough for Trevor and he had needed more. Sort of survivor guilt, it was easier to blame yourself than accept that some men were just shit. Then came the self-preservation and justifying it by trying to believe that she had been duped by him. But never, ever had I thought that she had led him on, that was loyalty. Besides, she had never pinched a fella from me before. In my eyes, it was one of those taboo things that mates, real mates, just didn't do.

Whatever, there was no way of finding out now. Any hopes that I might have had of reconciliation were buried on Mars. So now I could choose to blame Trevor without fear of contradiction. And if I chose to blame him, then revenge had to figure in my mind.

"Are we all ready then," said the man himself, he had graced us with his presence, large as life and twice as sickening. Seeing him coming towards me, all brash and full of himself made me even surer that he was manipulating me into doing what he wanted. I still hated his guts, over it all was the numbing grief that the reason I was going was to see someone who wasn't there. I had to get myself organised or I'd be no blooming use to anyone.

In a final attempt to stop going round in circles I tried to put it all together; was my real reason for coming on this little jaunt an attempt to make sure that I could pin it all on Trevor? He had been with her and she had died. Surely he was at least partly responsible, whatever he said; maybe it was wishful thinking but it kept me going.

But as Cy pointed out, Trevor was paying and we could do with a holiday. "I hear the food on the shuttle is really expensive," he said, "and I'm pigging out, on his bill, just to teach him a lesson."

The two of them had never got on, even when the four of us were working together. Trevor had always sneered at Cy, he was not subtle in his homophobia. Personally, I reckoned that Cy was more of a man because he had the guts to be what he wanted and say 'sod off' to everyone else. Trevor never put his money where his mouth was, so to speak; he kept it at low-level antagonism, niggling comments and behaviour, never enough on its own to be too much but the cumulative effect was corrosive.

"How do you put up with it?" I once asked him. His reply surprised me, I'd never thought of him as that sort of person.

"I'll get my chance one day to shaft him properly, pardon the expression. When I do I want him to see it coming and I want him to know, deep down, that there is absolutely nothing he can do, nowhere to run and hide. If I went for him he's the type to scream for his mummy to help him, failing that the law would probably do. So I'll do it differently, not give him a way out, he'll have to face it, and me."

Maybe he thought that this was his chance; maybe that was why he hadn't put up much of a fight about coming with me.

God, it was all so complicated; what should have been a straightforward expression of grief and sadness was in danger of turning into a vendetta.

They called us for the shuttle and after hugs all around we walked down the ramp. Ahead of me, through the panoramic view offered by the observation windows, I could see the shuttle, sitting moored to the magnetic clamps at the end of the tubular walkway. It looked like a green caterpillar with the row of lights shining along its length. There were a couple of suited figures working on the engine's assemblies around the tail. I had done that, seeing them there I could hardly believe it myself, it was a long way from dressmaking. I was proud of what I had achieved and contemplated telling Trevor. He thought that I was just a café owner; sod it, I'd tell him!

"I do that," I said, pointing.

"She does," added Cy. I thought Trevor might be impressed.

"What, you?" he sneered. "In a space suit, out there, yeah right, Andi. What do you do, take the tea and biscuits out?"

Clearly, I was wasting my time. I watched for a moment. The guys were manipulating hoses, either refuelling or charging the atmosphere. It was a weird job, when you tried to move something in Zero Gee, unless you were anchored it just sat there and you moved in the opposite direction. It took a bit of getting used to. Like the fact that there was gravity here, but fifty feet away there wasn't. I still hadn't grasped how that one worked.

Compared to the mining Scoopers I had been driving the shuttle was enormous, big enough for twenty passengers and a crew of six or seven. There was a spare in the hangar where the Scoopers lived. Tina, my instructor and friend, had told me that it was as simple to fly as a Scooper but it looked so daunting that I had never even considered it.

Had it really been just six months since I had pulled my suitcase in the other direction? I couldn't say that I was thrilled to be going back to Mars. I'd hated it the first time and that was without Trevor or the knowledge that my best friend was a victim of something unknown on that inhospitable red rock.

Chapter 3

I'd forgotten just how far it was from the station around Saturn to Tharsis on Mars. The shuttles arrived and left every week and that was all the thought I ever gave it. At least it was quicker than the first colonists, who had taken months to reach Mars from Earth. Coming up from Mars had been about four days, as far as I could remember.

And I was having a problem working out why our route included a stop above Earth. I was pretty sure that Mars and Saturn were both further away from the sun than the Earth was so why were we going from Saturn to Mars via Earth? I remembered a picture of the solar system from school with the planets in a line and I was sure that it was Earth, Mars, the asteroid belt, Jupiter and then Saturn.

The whole thing had started to make my brain hurt when the in-flight announcement before departure had said that it was four days to Earth and then three more after that before we got to Mars.

Just in case I was completely stupid and up to my usual trick of proving it to everyone with a dozy question, I waited until after the briefing. Trevor had gone to the loo and me and Cy were alone. I told him about my confusion and he laughed so much I thought he would never stop.

"What, Cy?" I pleaded. "Why can't I get it?"

"Listen," he said, "you're right about the order of the planets but they don't stay in a line like that as they orbit the sun. And the distances between them are not like in the picture either. If it was to scale the page would need to be about a mile long to get them all in. Because of the distances they are from the sun, Mars takes just under two years to go around once but Saturn takes twenty-nine years for an orbit."

Ahh, it was starting to sink in. It wasn't me that was wrong but the picture. So I wasn't mad after all. But Cy was in full flow, he sounded like Lou or Terri in the observatory, bent over a screen full of science. I got the meaning of the odd word here and there and nodded, like one of those toy dogs you used to see years ago.

"Because of that, the planets all end up in different relative positions; Mars is on the opposite side of the sun to Saturn at the moment. So, as we have to fly past the sun to get to it and as it's not that far out of the way, so to speak, we can stop at Earth. In about eight months, Mars and Saturn will be much closer and you won't go via Earth, in fact, the Earth will be on the opposite side of the sun then and it would be a major detour."

Ah, now that he put it like that I understood, sort of. I was relieved that I had asked him and not Trevor, or shouted out a question during the safety briefing. He gave me a hug. "Don't worry, a lot of people just can't take in the size of the place."

The fact that we could go zipping around the solar system in a matter of days was due to the development of the Centi-drive, so called because it could propel ships at up to around one per cent of the speed of light. Don't ask me how it worked; I might be a Scooper pilot but anything more technical than knowing which button to press was well above my capacity. But I was trained to shove corks into holes in the hull if the Scooper sprung a leak!

I had grasped the fact that we would be moving faster than a speeding whatever but it still took ages to get anywhere. After Cy had explained the position thing to me, I took an interest in the information we had been given when we boarded the shuttle. I found out that light took about eighty minutes to get from Saturn to Mars on average, at one per cent that was eight thousand minutes by Centi-drive or just under six days once you allowed for speeding up and slowing down. It made me realise that space was seriously big. And that was just our backyard, so to speak, how about if we wanted to go to another star?

Trevor returned. "I'm back," he announced, as if he needed congratulating for finding his way from the loo to the lounge on a shuttle; even I could do that on a good day. We both ignored him. His return had stopped us from discussing our tactics for the journey and how we intended to pass the trip in such close proximity.

The safety briefing had finished; we would be departing shortly and there was no reason for us to be confined together in the lounge. A buffet was laid out in the restaurant and we helped ourselves. I was surprised at the quality, considering the size of the galley it was a masterpiece of organisation. The three of us ate in a sort of strained silence, punctuated by monosyllabic exchanges.

I was trying to think how I could avoid Trevor without being too rude and it looked to me like Cy was trying to control his animosity.

My preferred method was by staying in my cabin as much as possible, although this would be difficult. True to his word he had bought return tickets in single cabins for me and Cy, but he had a double for himself and somehow I doubted his claim that "it was all they had." Ulterior motive could have been his middle name.

"If you were a gentleman," Cy said, "you would let Andi have the double and take her single cabin."

"I'd love to but I can't," Trevor replied. "Safety regulations, it's registered to me. We could always share it though."

"I can't," I answered, "safety regulations." He looked puzzled. "Avoiding hazardous situations; I might murder you!"

"The same goes for me," muttered Cy. Trevor squirmed, he was uncomfortable with Cy's sexuality and Cy had always loved to embarrass him with it. Just another way of getting his own back.

Trevor tried again. "Well you could just pop in after we've eaten. I need to fill you in on the background."

I was saved from answering as the tannoy system burst into life. "This is Captain Janes," said a deep voice. "While you enjoy your meal we are departing on our way to Mars, via Bravo Station above

Earth. Our estimated journey time to Earth orbit is just under four days. Enjoy your trip and if there is anything we can do, please don't hesitate to ask."

Looking out of the ports, I saw the station move rapidly away, yet felt no acceleration.

"Well," said Trevor, "are you coming over?"

"No need to be pushy," I said. "We've got six days to decide what we're going to do. I've got a headache. I'll leave you two to it and see you in the morning." I went to my cabin and locked myself in.

As I sat there on the cramped bed in my tiny box, I thought about Derek and our parting. I was missing him already. I had gone up to the farm to see him just as soon as I could get away. When I blurted out my news, that I was leaving for an unspecified time, over the death of someone he had never heard me mention, he was a bit surprised, to say the least.

"So why did you never mention this Maisie, if she was your best friend?" he asked as we sat outside on his terrace, drinking the slightly illegal wine that he made. "You're flying over eight hundred million miles to help her boyfriend after her suicide which you say might not have been and I've never heard you mention either of them before today."

"It's a long story," was all I could think of to say. It must have seemed a bit weird. If I had told him everything he probably would have had me fitted for one of those nice white jackets with buttons all the way up the back! He looked at me, it wasn't fair, I had to give him more than that.

"Trevor and Maisie were old friends of ours from London, we all worked together then we had a falling out. It was a big argument and I wanted to forget, to start over. That's why we came here. I was shocked when Trevor turned up and when I heard the news I knew that although we could never make up, this was the least I could do to try and put things right."

Derek got up and came to stand behind me; he put his arms around my shoulders, burying his head in my hair. I felt his hot breath on the back of my neck and lifted my hands to touch his arms. "Then she was lucky to have a friend like you," he said. "Of course you should go." I stood and kissed him.

"Thank you," I said as he led me off the terrace to walk around the fields of wheat and corn.

We stopped strolling and embraced; I was starting to feel a bit weepy about leaving him, especially as I hadn't been completely honest and he had been so understanding. I knew that he had his own reasons for not wanting me to go to Mars.

His wife had left him and gone to Mars before we had met. His daughter Davina was in prison on Mars, it had been me who had helped to put her there. That might have been enough to make him hate me; fortunately, he hadn't seen it that way.

The fact that I was going to the place where they both were can't have been easy for him to take, he had already said that he wouldn't go to visit Davina in case he saw Helen and I could understand his reluctance. At least he didn't know the whole story of that as well. What he did know was enough for anyone to take.

He knew that Davina had killed two people and had tried to escape using me as a hostage. What he didn't know and must never know, was that his wife had only left him because she had been pregnant with the child of some unknown man on the station. That was what had driven Davina to do what she had done. I hated keeping secrets, largely because I was no good at it, but so far I had managed to avoid giving the game away. Anyway, we didn't know who the mystery man was and we weren't intending to find out.

We finished our walk and went back to his living quarters, the ones we shared, and had dinner; there was something he wanted to ask, I could feel it. I didn't want to force him so I let it lie, it had to be one of two things, each would cost him, one of them could finish us. So I kept quiet and concentrated on making happy memories that would have to last both of us for a while.

"Come back soon," Derek said, in the early morning when the alarm told us that it was time for me to go. We held each other tight, just as we had all night. "And be safe."

He was so trusting; I realised that I had fallen in love, not the sort of love that I had felt with Trevor, I knew now that was more lust than anything and it wasn't really a surprise that it had burnt itself out. No, this was the real thing and it was much better.

I slept, dreaming that we were together again as the shuttle accelerated away from the station.

Next morning I met up with Cy at breakfast, Trevor hadn't shown yet. Neither of us could sleep after six, it came from getting up early to open the café. Cy told me that after I had gone to bed, to help keep me from being worried, or tempted, he had arranged with Trevor for the three of us to meet in his cabin to discuss tactics.

"That's sweet. Thanks, Cy," I said as we tucked into a breakfast that we hadn't had to cook ourselves for the first time in ages. "I appreciate it but I think I'm over him now."

He looked unconvinced. "Maybe, but let's make sure of it." He chewed for a while. "Have you wondered where the money's coming from to finance all this?"

It hadn't crossed my mind up to then. I guess I'd been concentrating on other things but, thinking about it, he was right. Trevor had agreed quickly, we hadn't really had to fight that hard to get him to pay for both of us. "Perhaps it's from some sort of insurance settlement, maybe he feels guilty."

"Could be, but I bet he's only paying cos he thinks he'll get more back. I'm going for all the extras, room service, the works." He poured more coffee and reached for the toast.

The flight wasn't crowded for the leg from the station to Earth; there were only five passengers, us and an older couple who I knew vaguely from the café. They were off to see their grandchildren on Earth. Now that I could understand that Mars was on the opposite side of the sun at the moment I could see the logic in stopping in Earth orbit for passengers and mail. We were chatting about the changes they would see, both in the planet and in their family, before Trevor breezed in and proceeded to hijack the conversation.

"Right then, what are we doing today?" he practically shouted, the woman of the couple rolled her eyes and made 'talk to you later' noises.

"Trevor," I said, "I'm talking to these people."

"But we have things to discuss," he said.

"How about we start with politeness?" suggested Cy. "We're eating and chatting to our fellow travellers, so when we've finished that, we can talk to you."

Trevor backed down; he turned to the couple. "I'm sorry," he said. "My life is a bit of a mess at the moment, please excuse me."

They smiled sympathetically but as Trevor turned to get some coffee, I saw the man make a rather uncomplimentary gesture. I couldn't help laughing. Cy saw it too.

"What's funny?" Trevor asked; he had his back to the couple.

"I've got to hand it to you," Cy said with a straighter face than I could have managed, "your job must pay really well if you can afford to jerk us off the station and pay for all this." That was it; I was almost hysterical at that point and the man was rolled up, the lady's face was a picture.

"You're all weird," Trevor said, sometimes other people could be as slow as me.

He sat. "What's your cabin like?" he asked. As if it would be different to his, except smaller! They were all only a bunk and a washroom, designed for sleep and a private area to wash and dress. Most of the space on the shuttle that wasn't devoted to fuel, oxygen and the other things that would keep us alive was taken up by the lounge and restaurant. Underneath the public space was the cargo compartment, at the front the crew quarters and stores. The galley may have only been small but it was more than capable of producing top quality food, helped by the supplies picked up from Derek's farm.

"It's OK," I said, not wanting to start the whole double argument again, he was quiet after that.

Our trip progressed, the day punctuated by announcements from the crew, things like 'we passed the orbit of Jupiter' and other technical stuff, I spent the time reading all the magazines that the shuttle had brought up from Earth, all the latest gossip and trivia. It was nice to get them before the throng on the station and have the time to look at them properly.

I know that I should have been taking more of an interest in our destination and what we were going to do. This was the first real break I'd had for a long while and I wanted a day of it before reality seeped back in.

But by that evening, I was gossip-columned out and when Cy reminded me of our meeting over dinner, I was as ready as I would ever be to face the reality. So after a shower, I went to his cabin. It was still a single but it was a bit larger than mine for some reason. It meant that he could sit between us. Cy knew that I had a fatal flaw with Trevor; he was making sure that I didn't succumb. I was slightly miffed; never mind Trevor swapping, why hadn't he offered?

Cy had ordered from room service, even though we hadn't long finished eating. I was about to tackle him about the swapping thing when he explained. "I thought it would make good neutral ground," he explained. "Honest, Andi, if I had taken yours then we would be in your personal space together. Here we can spread out a bit and I can keep you two apart."

I understood, this way I could keep Trevor from getting his foot in my door. It was a good idea but thankfully my ardour was cooling. I had come to realise that while I might have fancied him once, I hated him for what he had done to me and what he might have done to Maisie. Almost as soon as we had set off his attitude had changed, almost as if it was mission achieved getting me on board. It was like he thought, 'you're here now and I'm in charge, you probably still find me attractive and I'm going to use that to get what I want.' I could see through it, I knew then that I wouldn't need chaperoning any more.

There was a knock at the door. "Come in," Cy mumbled around a vol-au-vent. Trevor entered.

"Where am I going to sit?" he asked. Cy and I had nabbed the bed.

"You could sit on the toilet and leave the door open," suggested Cy, it would have suited him; he chose not to.

"I'll sit on the deck then."

Cy shrugged and turned his attention back to the food that he had ordered in an attempt to screw Trevor for as much money as we could. There were battered prawns on skewers, bite-size pieces of chicken in pastry, samosas, all sorts of salad.

We sat in silence, broken only by Cy masticating, his hand and his mouth in perfect harmony.

"What have you got there?" Trevor looked aghast at the plate that Cy was rapidly emptying. I had seen the prices of extras like these on the room service menu so I could sympathise. Little did he know that I would be having the same later, even though I was full of dinner, as a before sleep snack. "Do you know how much they cost?"

"Yes," said Cy. "You said you were paying, is that a problem?"

Trevor shook his head, even though you could feel his pain.

Cy stopped chewing for a second. "OK, fill us in with a bit more detail than yesterday."

"We had an apartment in Tharsis," Trevor began. "A nice one, Maisie was working in one of the old folks' homes, she had got herself qualified as a nursing assistant to make a few extra credits and for something to do."

That sounded like her, always caring for others. I swiped a prawn from Cy's plate and he swatted at my hand. Too late, I crunched the crispy batter it was cooked in; it was delicious.

"How long had you been on Mars?" I asked. It had been a year since I had last seen either of them. A year ago, there had been the falling out and me and Cy had left London on the journey that would take us to the Oort Cloud Café.

"Eight months," he said.

"Why go to Mars?" Cy joined in, talking around a mouthful of samosa. Flaky pastry fluttered and Trevor pulled a disgusted face.

"We both wanted a change," he said. "London was… not the same as it had been." He sounded surprised. As if all that could have happened and things had somehow remained the same.

"Carry on then," I encouraged him, before either of us got all maudlin.

"There was one old bloke she really got on with," he continued. "He used to be some sort of celebrity on Earth, I never found out what. Anyway, that was when he was working, now he was old and knackered. He seemed to have money though, the home wasn't cheap and he had a private suite and a personal chef. Maisie did lots for him, washed him, helped him get around, she gave him his drugs, all the usual stuff. The day before she…" he stopped as the memory made him well up. "The day before, he told her something important. She said that it was going to make her very rich."

"What was it?"

"She never said. I was asleep when she came in that night, she was on late shifts and I only found out in the morning, I was running late and she said that she would tell me all about it when she got back that night. She was really excited; it was her last shift before a few days off. I said I'd wait up, cook her a meal."

How romantic, he had never cooked me a meal.

"I thought that maybe he would be leaving her something in his will, I don't know; she said that he had no-one. And then the next thing I know, I'm at work, it's mid-afternoon and the care home is on the phone asking if she was sick because she hadn't turned up."

"How did they find her?" Cy asked.

"The locator on her phone," he said. "It showed that she was outside. I called the police and after they found it they sent a vehicle. On the way to her signal, they found her Rover, it was empty. They carried on and saw her sitting up against a rock, fully suited. It was only when she didn't answer that they got her into their Rover and found that her oxygen was empty."

There were so many questions I wanted to ask. I'd be better off making a proper list but I'd let him finish first.

"She looked so peaceful, like she would wake at any moment. The doctor examined her and said that she was full of sleeping pills. She would have been asleep well before the oxygen ran out."

Cy popped another canape into his mouth and made appreciative noises, Trevor winced. "Do you have to keep doing that?"

Cy looked at him. "No disrespect," he said, "but I'm hungry. Did she go outside a lot?"

"A few times, she wanted to see the rock formations at a place called Hensens Ridge, apparently they're beautiful, one of the other nurses was telling her about them. You can go and camp in a plastic dome or something but she said it would be more fun if we didn't go on the organised tour, just did it ourselves."

"Did you go with her?"

He shook his head. "No, I've been really busy with work and I never got the chance, with her on shifts she often worked weekends and had days off in the week. But I promised her that I would go when she was fully certified. Lately, we had hardly been seeing each other. I think she was going out for something to do." He looked sad. "I've made a mess of things haven't I?" he said in a whisper. "I didn't pay her enough attention."

Probably, I thought, but that didn't mean that Maisie would just go off and kill herself, there had to be more to it than that. I could see that Cy was about to remind Trevor of some of the things he had done to me in his pursuit of money, Trevor felt the energy as well.

"So to start with, we need to know what the man told her," I suggested, trying to defuse the tension. Although it seemed unlikely, maybe he had set off a train of thought that had made her slip up, do something dozy like I would have. Or maybe… no, that was too silly.

"He's on his last legs," said Trevor harshly. "That's why I had to rush you back so we can speak to him before he croaks. They wouldn't let me see him; maybe you'll have more luck." He sounded arrogant, less in grief than entitled, as if the man had insulted him by refusing to share. He made it seem like the poor old man was acting selfishly by being close to death.

"Perhaps if you'd been polite and asked nicely?" suggested Cy. I thought that was a bit provocative. Trevor gave him a look but didn't react.

"Is there anything you're not telling me, Trevor?" I didn't like the sound of this, I could smell fish and it wasn't the prawns on their dainty skewers, it was a great big rancid old cod dumped in the middle of the cabin. I liked it less and less as I found out more. The way he had been all over me until he had got what he wanted, his attitude in general, it was starting to grate.

He looked at me. "No, Andi. I swear I just want to know the truth, so I can put her to rest in my mind. The police organised the funeral and all the paperwork, I couldn't cope with dealing with the solicitor. If I thought for one moment that it was my fault, do you think I would come to you, the one person who would blame me, who already blames me?"

That was a fair point; the blame bit was about the only thing he had said so far that I could rely on.

"Alright then, but if I find out that you haven't told me the whole story, I'll make you sorry."

"I'm already sorry," added Cy, crunching another prawn.

Chapter 4

I was eating breakfast on the second day, we had two more to go to Earth orbit and already it was visible as more than a point; it was now a small ball off to one side of our bow. Cy and Trevor hadn't appeared, the trouble was that I was now so used to getting up early that I couldn't switch into holiday mode. The stewardess, Jess, brought me more toast and as she placed it by my side she said that she thought she recognised my face. "Excuse me," she said, "but aren't you the Andorra Pett who was in the news?"

Oh great, could I not get away from the fame, or was it the notoriety of my deeds?

"Yes," I said with what I hoped was a long-suffering sigh. Surely I wasn't going to have to tell it all again?

"Thought so," she replied. "Don't worry, it's not what you think, the pilot recognised your name from the paperwork, he wondered if you'd like a look around the flight deck after breakfast?"

To be honest, it wasn't really my thing. I enjoyed flying a Scooper but this would be so far over my head that I would have no chance of appearing remotely intelligent. And then I realised it would keep me out of Trevor's way for a few hours. Surely I could bluff my way through it if I kept that in mind.

"I'd love to," I answered with what I hoped sounded like enthusiasm.

"The flight crew are doing daily reports," she said. "When they've finished I'll come and find you."

Trevor appeared at that moment. "Hello," he greeted me, "we've got all day. You can tell me about how you caught that murderer."

Hah! Lucky escape time. "Sorry, Trevor, I'm on a promise," I replied smugly. He gave me a strange look as Cy arrived. We ate in silence for a while.

Cy had just finished his heart-attack-on-a-plate when Jess came back over. "Ms Pett, would you care to come with me?" I smiled triumphantly at Cy as I left him to it.

We went through a small door at the side of the room, Jess opened it with a security card. We walked down a narrow alleyway, past several cabins and a separate lounge. The last door was marked 'Lavatory'. I remembered a problem I'd had once confusing Lavatory with Laboratory. Perhaps I could tell the flight crew about it if there was a lull in the conversation, as long as they weren't eating. Ahead was a door that announced itself as 'Flight Deck, Authorised Personnel Only'. It also opened to her card.

"In you go," said Jess. "I've got to get back to work. Rufus is in there, he'll look after you."

The flight deck was what I had expected; a bit like an airliner in layout, cramped for space with three seats, two at the front with a view of the heavens and one on the side with a view of rows and rows of switches, read-outs and gauges. And Tina had reckoned I could fly one of these?

The front left seat was occupied. The pilot got up; he was tall and good looking. "Hello, Ms Pett," he said in the same deep bass voice I'd been hearing on the tannoy. "I'm Rufus Janes, it's a pleasure to meet you." He held out his hand and I shook it.

"Are you on our own in here?" I blurted out, oh dear, another bad start. He was another one, a man who made me gabble.

He laughed. "It's quite safe, they do let me sit here on my own sometimes. Anyway, the automatic is driving."

Once again the wrong words had come out, that wasn't what I had meant to say, or mean. I didn't want to be rude, maybe I should try and explain. That would probably get me deeper in trouble so instead I changed the subject.

"It's very different to a Scooper." If I could talk about what I knew, I might be alright.

He laughed again. "I learnt to fly on a Scooper," he said, "on the station, way back when."

Well at least we had common ground and something that I could talk knowledgeably about. "What did you think of the simulator?" I asked.

He laughed. "Bloody Tina, I barfed almost before you could say push the wheel forward."

I laughed with him. "She's a nightmare. She never told me that the crew in operations would be watching."

"The vomit comet," he said.

I'd managed to hold onto my breakfast when I'd been in there; it gave me a feeling of superiority. "So how easy would it be to fly this?" Tina had told me it was no different, I couldn't believe it.

"Sit there," Rufus said, pointing to the right-hand seat. "That's the co-pilot's seat. I'm afraid that you can't sit in my seat." I felt slighted, why couldn't I sit in the captain's seat?

"Why? Is that because you're the captain and it's the captain's seat?"

He laughed again, why was my every utterance funny?

"No, I'm taller than you and the seat's pushed right back. You couldn't sit on it and reach the controls. And I've got to sit somewhere."

Oh, was that all? Calm down, Andi. I sat down and got myself comfy. There were two pedals and the wheel arrangement, just like on the Scooper. That was it. A few more switches and dials but not many. "Well," Rufus raised an eyebrow, "what do you think, is there any difference?"

"There are two pedals."

"Ah, you spotted that, one's for the ordinary drive and the other one's for the Centi-drive."

"Couldn't you have one pedal for both and a switch?" I asked.

"Well we could have a switch, I suppose," he said. "But then we would need to remind the engineer to turn it." He looked and sounded so serious that I almost fell into the trap of answering. There must be another reason. Perhaps it was a secret, maybe it wasn't a pedal at all, just a footrest.

"So, did you get fed up with Scooping? How come you ended up here?"

"Yeah, this is a step up alright. I'm not getting pelted by rocks all day and arguing about tonnage when I should be resting. All I have to do is monitor the automatic and do the odd landing, just to keep my hand in." It looked like I wouldn't be doing any driving after all. Maybe that was a good thing.

It sounded like a nice arrangement; I could imagine myself doing this for a job. "How many crew are there, I've only really seen the cook and the stewardess?" I asked.

"There are five; two pilots, an engineer, a cook, and a stewardess, but we all do a bit to help out. I do some cooking and Jess is a qualified electrician. And the cleaning is all done between us, or left for the ground crew." Impressive, I wondered if they needed a dressmaker, they already had someone who could do everything that I could.

"So is it all automatic?"

"It can all be done remotely; we're only here in case of an emergency and to monitor the life support. All the stuff on that panel over there is for the passenger compartment. If anything goes wrong with the drive we'll just keep everyone alive until the rescue party turns up."

"Where are the corks?"

"We've gone a bit past corks," he said. "The hull is self-sealing, there's a liquid layer in between the two metal skins. If it's exposed to vacuum it solidifies."

It sounded like clever stuff, but probably more expensive than a box of corks. And dead passengers were harder to explain away than dead miners.

"And we have a force field to keep particles away," he added. Now I was sure he was winding me up.

"Oh yeah," that sounded a bit unlikely. "How does that work then?"

"Electrostatic repulsion, you must have seen the bumps on the hull?"

Now that he mentioned it, I had noticed them. The trouble was, he was so straight-faced, he could have told me anything and I would have believed him. But I reckoned I was doing OK so far. Then I asked the dozy question.

"Why aren't we heading straight for Earth?"

"Because it's moving relative to us, we're heading to where it will be when we get there."

I knew that, of course I did!

The door opened and two men came in; it was getting crowded in here. "This is Grant, the co-pilot and Ryan the engineer," said Rufus. "Guys, this is Andi Pett, the lady from the station."

There were hellos from the two. "I'm in your seat," I said and started to get up.

"No that's fine, you stay there," said Grant. "I'm only here to pick up my job sheet for today. Anyway, you're famous; I can tell everyone that Andorra Pett sat in my chair."

"I thought you were a bloke," said Ryan, going rapidly downhill in my estimation.

"Get back to monitoring the sewage tank," said Rufus, without malice.

"Yeah but only to start with," Ryan's voice was pained, as if he had been saying that for a while. "We all did, if I remember correctly."

"Well if you did then you're not the only ones," I said, I liked them, they were a crew, a unit, if the cook was the same then with Jess they made a good team.

"Why are you going to Mars, Andi?" said Grant. "If you don't mind my asking? Are you on a case?"

Oh marvellous, could I not go anywhere now without that question? People weren't asking it when I went to the loo but just about every time I was somewhere on the station that wasn't the café someone would ask me what I was up to.

"No, not me. I'm going to Mars to help out a friend."

The three exchanged knowing glances. I wasn't selling it. OK I was investigating but it was personal this time, I didn't have a murderer to catch, just some answers to get.

"Tell us about how you worked out what was going on back on the station. When you caught the murderer," Grant said. "We read the news but they always get it wrong."

I didn't really want to but then I thought, hey it keeps me away from Trevor.

"OK, get some tea in here and I'll tell you all about it."

Chapter 5

Cy was furious and I mean furious, he wasn't joking. "You bitch!" he said when I finally reappeared in the lounge, his face was red and he acted like he was having trouble stopping himself from strangling me. "I've been stuck with him all bloody day. I've had three showers just to get away from him."

"Sorry, Cy, the crew wanted to chat and I couldn't get away." He scowled at me.

"I bet you tried really hard too!"

"Listen, calm down, I've set it up, they want to talk to you as well, tomorrow. They didn't realise it was you with me, we've got tea and biscuits with them after breakfast in the crew lounge. Jess will call us when they've finished all their routine stuff."

He brightened up a bit at that. "And then we're arriving at Bravo station," he said, "and it's only two more days after that."

"I was thinking," I said, "if we talk really slowly, I reckon we could make it last."

"Do... you... know," he said, dragging the words out, "I... think... we... could!"

"Where have you been?" asked Trevor at dinner. "The shuttle's only so big and I couldn't find you anywhere. I've only had Cy to talk to all day."

"Don't I know it," he muttered, not quite under his breath.

"Sorry, Trevor," I said. "I got chatting to the crew. The captain's an ex Scooper pilot and we've been talking shop, I lost track of time."

"Anyone would think you were avoiding me. At least Cy has been keeping me company; we've had a good old chat."

That wasn't quite what I'd heard. Just you wait till tomorrow morning, I thought.

We had to eat together. Trevor was flirting with Jess. I expect she was used to it from the passengers because she handled him easily and politely. "My boyfriend's a big martial arts fan," she said as he clumsily tried to get her talking about sport. "He's always practising." That shut him up

I made an effort and spent the mealtime talking to Trevor, he asked about the station and we gave him an idea of what it was like. When I described the Scoopers and things that I had done, he seemed a bit dubious and I found myself asking Cy to back me up.

After we had eaten, Cy cleared off but I couldn't really complain.

"So how did you catch this murderer?" he asked me, as we sat in the lounge with coffee. The old couple were opposite us and when Trevor wasn't looking they shot me sympathetic glances. It was OK though; he had turned on the charm and was the same easy to talk to person that he had used to be.

"I get the idea that you don't think that I can do what I said." I tackled him head on.

"It's not that," he said. "It's just that Maisie said that you could and I rubbished her. It makes me feel bad to hear that she was right."

"Well it was easy," I started. Then I remembered what I couldn't say. I couldn't tell him about the book, or anything about Derek's wife or anything about Mike. Cy and I had gone through how to explain it without mentioning any of those things. We had to blame Munro and mention a few clues to justify our working it all out. As Munro was dead, we could pin it all on him, he couldn't answer back. It was the most useful he had been to us.

"There were lots of clues, the people that broke in were working for a dubious character, one was involved with the killer. We just pieced it all together."

Then Trevor went and spoiled it. "I expect Cy did most of the working out," he said.

I got up. "Goodnight, Trevor," I said.

"What, c'mon, Andi. I was only joking, I know you're clever really, don't be so thin-skinned."

Which didn't help, maybe it was best to get it all out in the open before we got to Mars.

"That's not the right thing to say, Trevor. Perhaps if I hadn't have been so thin-skinned I wouldn't have minded you shagging Maisie. Is that what you mean?"

He went pale and the old lady's ears pricked up. I walked out and went to sleep, but not before I'd had a good cry in the privacy of my cabin.

~~~~

Sure enough, Jess called us as we were relaxing after breakfast. Trevor had only just turned up and was tucking in, no doubt thinking he had us to talk at all day. I was waiting for him to apologise, it wasn't happening.

"Do you want to come up with me?" she said. "We'd love to," we both said at once and left Trevor sat there, with a forkful of bacon halfway to his mouth.

We had to repeat the whole story again to Rufus and the rest of the crew, it was easier with Cy. We could let each other do the talking and interrupt if it was getting too close to the real truth. Rufus and Grant knew who Munro was, so that bit was accepted, they filled the rest in on what they thought, which saved us the bother.

We spent the day with them and only emerged for dinner. Trevor looked ready to bite lumps out of the furniture when he saw us.

"Where have you been?"

"Out for a walk," said Cy. "Where do you think?"

"The crew wanted to talk to us about the station; they worked there, they wanted to know how everyone was."

"I've been sat here on my own all day," he whined, as if that would get him sympathy.

"What about the other passengers?"

"They won't talk to me."

"Perhaps you should try being polite."

~~~~

Somehow we all ended up in Cy's cabin after dinner. "Let's carry on from where we were last night," Trevor said.

"You're going to apologise then?"

"For what?" He could be as dense as me sometimes.

"For suggesting I was too thin-skinned to ignore you and Maisie."

"Oh that." He waved his arms about. "Yeah, sorry. But I'm in a state, can't you understand?"

"If you're going to try and turn it around and make it all about you," Cy got up from the bed, "then I'm going to bed."

"You can't," Trevor replied.

Cy looked at him. "Don't you tell me what I can't do. I'll do what I want."

Trevor was grinning. "You can't cos this is your cabin!"

Even I had to laugh at that.

Next morning we arrived in Earth orbit. We were only scheduled to be there for a few hours to pick up mail and a couple of passengers. Seeing the planet floating there, like a blue and white ball, made me feel homesick for London. At least I could go back there after all this was over without having to worry about seeing Trevor in my old haunts, now that he was based on Mars. And why had they gone to Mars, had it been his idea or hers?

That got me thinking; what about the money? Had Trevor got it all? What had happened to my share from the house? And what about my sister, Argentia? A half of the house was hers. Had she got her share? I'd have to find out. If he had spent it all there would be trouble, not just from me either. And it would be no good blaming Maisie, just because she wasn't there.

We docked at Bravo platform of the Orbiting Livestock Company. They were now owned by the mining station and were Derek's employer. And my landlord.

There was the chance to get off the shuttle and have a walk

around the platform but I couldn't be bothered. Trevor went though, he said that he wanted to stretch his legs and make a few calls. It was a relief to see the back of him, if only for a while. The three of us being together in such close proximity had resulted in a lot of tension and I was sick of it. I think that Cy was too.

We sat in the shuttle's lounge and they piped the TV onto the big screen. I listened with half an ear as Cy told me about how he and Trevor were bickering about our living arrangements once we got to Tharsis.

I was just about to say that I thought we had agreed that we would be going into a hotel when I was shocked to find that the main character from one of my favourite soaps was in a wheelchair! How had that happened? I had missed about a thousand episodes and most of the other people were unknown to me. I was just starting to catch up when it ended. Now I'd never find out. Then the news came on.

There was the usual gloom and doom about politics, at least wars were absent, ever since space exploration had ramped up with the Centi-drive there was a greater spirit of co-operation in the world. Which was not to say that there was no violence, it was just small scale; very local and like a lot of things had been taken out of government hands. But there was still plenty to bitch about. The station might have been many things, but at least it was free of political posturing and points scoring, mostly.

After the main news and the sport, which meant little to me anyway, there was the usual 'and finally' item. This one was about an old mystery that even I could remember, it had been news for months while I was at school.

"The last of the men connected with the Swissbank diamond robbery died this morning," the announcer said. "Jez Perrim was seventy-four and went to his grave never revealing the whereabouts of the stolen gems, taken in an audacious raid over twenty years ago. All the perpetrators were caught and received long sentences; the diamonds have never been recovered. One thing is certain, the stones must still be hidden somewhere."

Behind the announcer, film of the events surrounding the robbery played out. The co-anchor added with a chuckle, "They don't take up a lot of space; perhaps it's time to check in the back of all our cupboards, maybe one of us will get lucky." There was laughter and the news closed, replaced by adverts.

"Was that really twenty years ago?" said Cy. "That's before Mars was properly settled; there were only a few small bases on the moon then."

"And the station was only an idea; OLC had only just started the first platforms in Earth orbit."

It seemed so long ago, it was another world then, things had happened so quickly in the last few years.

Unfortunately Trevor made it back on board before we cast off to continue our journey. We had been joined by six elderly passengers for the trip to Mars. They monopolised the dining facilities, complained that the tea wasn't made properly and shouted at each other all the way. Jess worked herself into a frenzy catering for them and somehow managed to smile. If they had come into the Oort Cloud Café behaving like that I would have sent them all to Munro's diner, never mind the loss of business.

Munro's diner was still my competition on the station, it had survived the death of its owner and was now run by his widow. She had given up her job on the farm after his death and never missed the chance to blame me for that. As if it was my fault that her husband had been a criminal and manipulator of men. That he had just happened to be killed outside my place wasn't down to me. She should be careful; I knew things about her that I was sure she would hate to become public. Trouble was, I couldn't tell her, but the sight of her with her prim, superior attitude made me want to just say, "Do you remember when…?" to her sometimes.

The TV signal from Earth faded as we raced away, ahead was a close encounter with the sun, we would be using its massive gravity to slingshot us towards the point on its orbit where Mars would be when we got there.

We had run out of things to talk about with the crew and they were busy making sure we didn't crash into the sun anyway so we had to talk to Trevor.

"Which hotel are we staying in?" I asked him, remembering what he had said, how he hadn't arranged anything.

"The Metropol," he answered, he seemed happier after his walkabout. "I called from the platform and sorted it."

That was good news. "So we're not stopping at yours then?"

He shook his head. "No, I told you I'd get a hotel. I tried to book from the station before we left; there was no room in a lot of the hotels. I was on the cancellation list at the tourist office. I just called from the platform; they had found two rooms for you at the Metropol."

Put like that, it sounded reasonable, even plausible.

The rest of our journey passed in comfort. Trevor had stopped hassling me after it became clear even to him that things weren't going back to the way they were. I was over the feelings I used to have; they had been replaced by the nagging sensation that I had done the wrong thing, again. Then on the day before our arrival, we had a bit of fiddling around with the clocks to contend with.

Mars was keeping different time to us so we had to jump back from midnight to one in the afternoon twelve hours before we arrived. Why we couldn't have done it in stages over the journey I'll never know. I remembered that we had done the same thing on our way from Earth to Mars and again on the way from Mars to the station.

I asked Jess why, as she served us dinner; my stomach thought it should be breakfast.

"Time dilation," she said as if it was obvious, maybe it was to her. I just wished that I hadn't asked. At least I had had lots of practise appearing to know what was going on. "Oh go on then," I said. "Tell me all about it."

She frowned. "You're asking me! You're a pilot, I'm a stewardess.

I should be asking you."

Hmm, she obviously had this crazy idea that I actually knew about the mechanics of space flight and all that stuff, instead of just being a glorified sweeper-up.

"We don't do time dilation," I said. "Look, I just scoop rocks, we're not trained to do much else, not even navigation. We have a button to press when we want to go home."

She looked at me, I was sure she thought I was pulling her leg.

"Honest?" she said. "A button?"

"Yes, honest, so if I don't understand time dilation, please humour me."

"OK," she said. "Well, it all comes from Einstein; he proved that as you travel faster, time slows down for you but not for your destination."

So that was why it always took so long to get to the seaside when I was little, I knew there was a reason.

"So before we set the clock for Mars, we get an accurate readout of their time from their super-accurate master clock."

"Hang on a minute," I said, then I realised just how inappropriate the phrase was, Jess never noticed, "so how much are we talking about?"

"At one per cent light speed for six days, not much, maybe twenty seconds, but it's easier to do all the time changes in one go when we're twelve hours out. The maximum we would ever need to change is twelve and a half hours, half a Martian day. Otherwise we'd be altering a few hours every night. Earth time and Martian time are all different anyhow. We could be forward ten hours on the way from the station to Earth and back nine from Earth to Mars. It all depends on relative position."

"So that's why we didn't bother for the stop at the station above Earth."

"That's right. Did you notice the time on the TV was wrong?"

I hadn't but I was pleased to find that I had kept up with the explanation, mostly. The bit up to Einstein was crystal clear, the rest not so much, but it had raised one more question.

"OK, then if that's all true and I'm younger now than I would have been if I had stayed on the station, why is there no time lag in video calls?"

"Ahh, I do know that one. My fella on Earth is involved in the technology for that. Incidentally, he likes me getting younger every time I see him. Anyway, it's to do with Quantum Entanglement.

I didn't learn. I should have quit while Jess thought I was ahead. "Is that like that really cheesy old programme they keep repeating on the TV?"

"No, that's *Quantum Leap*! Entanglement has to do with the properties of photons from the same source, if you separate them by distance; they mimic each other's behaviour, instantly. So you can have one set on Earth and another on the station, if you modulate one the other copies it. And you can use that to send information, like radio waves."

It all sounded like a scam to me, I was getting younger by travelling faster but I could move something on Earth, and eight hundred million miles away something else would move instantly. Did I look daft?

"You know, Jess," I said.

"What?" she answered. She was probably expecting me to say how well she had explained it, or how I finally understood.

"Where I come from, they call that a whopper!" She gave me a funny look.

"I have to get on," she said as she practically ran away.

Whatever the truth of it was, I was sure that the old people on the trip would be pleased to have shaved a few seconds off on the way to their new homes.

All it meant to me was that I was tired and a bit grumpy when we landed and rolled into the huge hangar built into the side of a hill on Mars. Cy had been quiet, he wasn't a bad flier, just a bad lander. I remembered from our arrival here last time, he had been sick for most of the descent, at least he seemed to have been better this time.

I sat next to him and told him it would be would be fine. "It couldn't be worse than bouncing among the rocks in a Scooper and I've always got back from that," I said. And the thought seemed to help him.

Landing had not been exciting, there had been no real re-entry, or turbulence, the Martian atmosphere wasn't thick enough for that. Instead we had just spiralled down towards a cluster of lights in the desolation of the wilderness. From up high the planet looked flat and shadows distorted the shape of the mountains and valleys. Rufus kept us updated with all sorts of interesting information about the conditions on Mars, basically deadly, and the features we passed over, names of mountains and things that I would never remember, but as the night overtook us and it all went dark these snippets stopped.

All we could see now were the lights, getting closer. One hundred kilometres out, then fifty and the mountains began to take on a dark, looming mass. Twenty kilometres out and they were towering above the plains. Now there were lights above us as well as in front. Up ahead they pointed to a runway in the red earth and the wheels were lowered with a thump.

We swung in a wide circle over the lights. "We're just letting a flight from Earth land first," said Rufus and we could see the craft in the clear air, like a multicoloured dragonfly as it landed and taxied. Then it was our turn. We touched down with a rumble and a cheer from the passengers, kicking up a cloud of dust that shut out the view for a few seconds, it hung around us, there was little wind to move it on and we dragged it with us.

We slowed and taxied towards the hangar door, a vast piece of engineering that kept the dust out of the arrivals area. It opened as we got closer. The hangar itself, a large cave, was well lit and after the station, a huge open space.

Cy let go of my hand. "You know," he said, "I'm getting the hang of this space travel lark. Now I know that you do it all the time and it doesn't bother you I feel safer, if you know what I mean."

On the other side of me, Trevor, who I had been ignoring, snorted, "What she does isn't exactly like this."

Cy was on him, leaning over me. "She's got more balls than you," he said. "People DIE doing what she does. I'd like to see you do it." He was silent; mind you he had been almost non-existent for the last day or so, maybe now that he was almost home the reality of his situation was catching up with him.

The door closed behind us and that was it, we were in the heart of the Tharsis Ridge, in an old lava flow. The space wasn't airtight so we still had to walk down a sealed walkway and through an airlock. There was the familiar disinfectant spray and ultraviolet flash, like when we went into the farm on the station. The inner door opened and we were free to embark on the march to immigration. As we were all citizens of Earth these days I never really understood the need for immigration control any more, it wasn't like there was a separate gate for little green men or anything.

Perhaps the unions insisted, maybe it was health and safety. When we got there, out of about twenty gates only one was open. Staff lounged, watching the queue. Some things never changed. The other flight must have landed one of those corporate team bonding groups, there were about twenty of them in identical suits and they were all in front of us.

I showed my ID card and after my face had been compared to the picture I was allowed to walk another couple of miles to get my luggage. That was another thing that needed changing; why couldn't it all be in one place? And I didn't know anyone who looked remotely like their ID picture. At least I wasn't asked if I was that lady from the news, in fact I hardly seemed to have been noticed.

When we eventually got to Customs it was another wait. "Why are you coming to Mars?" the uniformed man asked me in a bored voice, when I finally got to the front of the queue. "My friend died, I'm here to pay my respects," I said. The official nodded, even though you could see that he hadn't really listened, he probably thought that my friend was one of the retired population. Perhaps he would have taken an interest if I told him that I'd come to blow all the nursing homes up. My bag was unpacked and inspected without comment.

We all got through the checks and were free to leave. The arrivals hall was festooned with advertisements for mobility scooters, golf courses and spa hotels. Trevor had been right; the place was turning into a retirement village. We had just arrived with another six to add to the throng. And the clock said that it was 24:31, which was just plain wrong.

Because of the time of day, or night, arrivals was quiet, just a few taxi drivers holding placards with names in large type, most were for Critical Holdings, whoever they were, the rest were on Care Home placards. Our fellow passengers flocked towards them, elbowing people out of the way

"I'll get you a cab to your hotel," Trevor said, he still seemed distant, but then, he was back to face the rest of his life here without her; everything, every place would have memories.

"I'm going back to my apartment," he said, "check the mail and that; I've been away from work for quite a while." I could imagine him walking into the rooms, they probably still had Maisie's scent in the air, maybe her stuff was scattered around. For a moment I almost felt sympathy.

He walked us to the cabs, a row of open-topped buggies, and helped us load our bags. "Metropol hotel," he said to the driver, handing him a card, which the man swiped through a reader, just like the till in the café.

"It's a nice hotel," he said. "Have whatever you want; it'll all go on the bill. I'll be over to pick you up at about nine in the morning. We can go to see the old man in the care home."

That was good news; at least we could have a rest before we did much, the last few days had been a Trevor overdose, despite the distractions I'd managed to find.

The cab drove from the port to the hotel through the tunnels that formed the city, it was a bit like the city of Petra back on Earth, only with a lid. I'd never been but I'd seen pictures, taken the 3D virtual reality tour. The source of the light was hidden behind some sort of reflectors, which gave a diffused glow like cloudy daylight. I remembered that it got darker and lighter, mimicking the length of the day. Only here the day was about an hour longer than it was on Earth. And Trevor was right; there were a lot of older people roaming about, even though it was the middle of the night.

My parents would have been long asleep by now, worn out by ill health and decades of physical struggle. Most of the folk we saw were on foot but there were a lot of those funny electric scooters as well. Some of them had been made up to look like motorbikes with huge handlebars and multiple mirrors.

The overriding red of the Martian rock had been toned down with imported plants in proper brown soil. Trees and bushes grew and I saw that weeds had sprung up in gaps and empty spaces. We were colonising Mars in more ways than one.

"Your first time on Mars?" asked the cab driver as he wove in and out of the tunnels. There were a lot more of them than I remembered; in fact the whole place had grown considerably in the months since we had left.

"No, we've been here before," answered Cy. I recognised a few places, the grandly named Main Street with its shops and cafés and the rows of box fronted apartments squeezed into the tunnels, all painted in clashing pastels, like seaside cottages.

"I was gonna tell you about the place," he continued, "but if you've been before I guess you know. It's funny, lots of people say they've been before and they just had to come back. That's the thing about this place, people love it so much they always come back." That was ironic, I hadn't wanted to come back. "And your friend, he's paying for everything, wow!"

"It's business," Cy said. "It'll all be on expenses."

The driver thought for a moment. "I've seen him around, you

see most people, there's only a few of us young'uns here, there must be money in whatever he does."

I could see that he was right. "There do seem to be a lot of old folk about," I said. "More than I remember from when we were here last."

"It's turning into a big business, the oldies," he said. "Something to do with the atmosphere and the lower gravity. Someone's making a killing," he laughed. "Is your friend an undertaker? That's the trade to be in. Mind you, I get lots of work from 'em taking them to the doctors or the hairdressers, or to the airlock for day trips out around the crater."

He suddenly hauled on the steering wheel; a mobility scooter had swung out in front of him. The violent change of direction made our buggy lift up onto two wheels. We just missed it and landed with a jolt. The horn blasted, but the other rider just carried on.

"It does mean that you get the blind and the deaf out and about," he said. "Sorry about that, they think that they own the tunnels, some of the ones on those bloody scooters."

The other difference that was immediately apparent was in the clothing. On the station it was all boiler suits and working gear, functional things, here it was jeans and tee shirts, shorts and beach wear.

We arrived at the hotel Trevor had chosen for us, the Tharsis Metropol. It wasn't shabby and clearly he hadn't been afraid to spend a few credits. Considering he had wanted us to stay at his, this was a result. The money for this was coming from somewhere, maybe it was guilt. Maybe he could afford it; for all I knew, he had landed a well-paid job. That would explain why he had changed his career from the accountant he had been on Earth.

We checked in and were taken to our rooms. "See you at breakfast," I shouted to Cy. His room was in a different part of the hotel and he went in a separate lift to me.

"Eight o'clock, I'll be there," he replied.

Chapter 6

My room was comfortable; the surprise was that there was a window. I would have thought that being underground they wouldn't have bothered, but no, there were heavy curtains and behind them a big pane of glass. Of course it was dark so you couldn't see what was behind it; there was just a dim outline of shapes in the gloom. I was tired and my body clock was out of synch. The bed was inviting and the bathroom was off to one side. I set my alarm for seven, which would be a two hour lie-in from the café and still give me time for a shower before breakfast. Unpacking my case I put my straighteners by the side of the bed. I brushed my teeth and put on my nightclothes. I think I was asleep almost before my head hit the pillow.

I had dreams, me and Trevor, then me and Derek. Maisie was in all of them, sometimes I was on Earth, sometimes on the station; their faces were all mixed up. It seemed logical in my dream that Maisie was alive and on the station, or that Derek was in the shop on Earth with me. Then Trevor and Derek had a fight, Maisie showed me a ring Trevor had bought her, a big sparkly diamond, I got angry. The usual muddle as my sleeping mind tried to process my waking moments.

When the alarm woke me the bedside light was still on and I had a headache. Without thinking, I plugged my straighteners in and went for a shower. It was a luxury to turn the taps and find that they didn't turn off immediately you let them go. There was water here, plenty of it and I prepared to enjoy a long shower. But I was so used to doing it quickly that I got bored and got out anyway. I dressed in a skirt and tee shirt; it felt strange after the boiler suits.

The last time I had worn a dress had been with Heynrik, and look what had happened there.

I was in the restaurant by eight but Cy had beaten me to it. Gone were the days when you needed a crowbar to get him out of bed.

"Are you weightlifting?" I said as we queued up for the buffet. He was piling his tray with at least one of every item that was on offer. All you can eat was a challenge to him, almost a command.

"Too right," he agreed. "I will make sure that this is the most expensive mistake that Trevor ever makes, bringing us here."

We carried our trays over to a table. I was having a pathetic breakfast compared to Cy, just juice, coffee and a few pastries against his heart-attack on two plates.

"I'll have to go back for coffee," he whinged. "I couldn't fit it on the tray."

I shook my head. "Perhaps if you hadn't had cooked *and* continental. Let's not forget that Maisie's dead in the stampede to bankrupt Trevor."

"Sorry," he muttered between mouthfuls. "You know, I really liked her until she betrayed you."

Cy had never liked Trevor, he had always thought that he was wrong for me but up to now I couldn't remember him having a bad word for Maisie.

"I prefer to think that Trevor did all the betraying," I said.

"It takes two," he replied.

"Well that's something I guess we'll never know then," I snapped. I didn't want an argument, it would do no good.

"Sorry," he said. "I'm not being very tactful, I'm tired and I didn't sleep well, next door was... noisy and I have a headache."

"You've got one too?"

"Yeah, I seem to remember it's something to do with the atmospheric pressure. It's different to that on Earth and on the station and it makes your head ache. We'll get used to it after a day or so."

"Have you worked out what we're going to do now that we're

here?" I said, in an attempt to change the subject. I hadn't really given it much thought. I suppose that Trevor must have had an idea and I guess that I was prepared to go along with it. Maybe I should be a bit more pro-active.

"Well, it depends on what the old man says I guess." He chewed for a moment. "And then there's the police investigation, there must have been one. They wouldn't just say suicide; that must be the official verdict. It would be nice to see what they based it on."

I had thought the same. "From what he told us, it sounds like suicide, but I think a more important question is why. Why did she suddenly go off, just when she had learnt that she would be rich?"

"So there are two questions already, I reckon we need to see a bit more of the place before we can work out if suicide was plausible. Things like the airlock and the vetting for when you hire a Rover. I don't understand the rush to get us out here. We could have read transcripts on the station and asked questions on a video link. Unless…"

"What, Cy?"

"Unless Trevor wants you here for something specific," he said.

"Oh!"

"Yeah, something that you have to do in person, or something that would only have a meaning to you when you saw or touched it."

If he was right, it reinforced the feeling in my stomach that there were things that I wasn't being told. "Maybe this old man has a message and will only tell me?"

"Then why didn't Trevor say that? Just that we had to get to him before he dies. Well, he's wasted at least a fortnight when we could have started looking the next day."

"We'll have to keep an eye out, he's up to something; we don't have the full story."

Trevor turned up just before nine. He was shaved and dressed in a smart suit. What did annoy me was the long blonde hair on his jacket. Maisie had always had dark brown hair. She had always wanted to be a blonde but couldn't use colours, they gave her a rash.

"All done?" he asked. We nodded. "Right then, I'll take you to the care home."

As we came out of the hotel, I saw a busy street, it was a lot brighter than last night and the absence of a single point of light made it look like a cloudy day. Did it ever rain? Maybe there were sprinklers up there with the lights. A scruffy kid was lounging by the bottom step, watched by the doorman. As I came out he started towards me, then he saw Trevor and backed off. He turned and ran. The doorman shook his fist at his departing back.

"Blooming kids, they pester the guests for money all the time," he said as we walked past him to the parking bays.

"Had any more thoughts?" Trevor said as we got into his car, one of the open-topped buggies. "If you can talk to this man he might be able to tell you what he told Maisie."

"Trevor, I've had six hours' sleep, my head hurts and I'm space lagged. My only thought is how quickly I can satisfy your guilt and get off this rock."

"Ditto," Cy added.

"Aww… come on, Andi, you said you'd help me. The headache will go, it's cos of the pressure in the tunnels, it affects your sinus and your ears. Hold your nose and blow, it'll help."

I tried it and he was right, although it wouldn't do to admit it.

It was time to find out about Trevor's plan. "Have you tried to see this man then?"

"I did pop in," he said casually. "I said that I wanted to thank him for his kindness to Maisie, some of the clients can be really rude but she said that he never was. The staff wouldn't let me see him; they said that it was family only."

"So how the hell do you think that I'm going to manage it?"

"You'll think of something, Andi, you always did." He started the buggy and lurched out backwards into the road. There was the blare of a horn, another vehicle was really close. Trevor changed gear and spun the wheel; we pulled away in a cloud of red dust which made us all choke. Either he was out of practice in the traffic or he wasn't concentrating.

"Are you trying to kill us?" Cy bellowed from the back seat.

"You have to just go, nobody stops to let you out," Trevor shouted.

I could see what he meant, the roads were very busy and there were a lot more vehicles about. Traffic lights and courtesy were certainly absent; I saw several near misses as we drove through the tunnels. There only seemed to be two main types of vehicle, those that were airtight and could go outside and open-topped ones like ours that were obviously only for interior use.

There was also a vehicle similar to the run-arounds that we had on the station only with a bigger load cage at the back. There were still a lot of mobility scooters weaving in and out with the sort of casual abandon that comes with old age. It was a bit like driving in Rome on acid, lots of beeping, shouting and waving.

We popped out of a small tunnel into a bigger space and pulled up outside a white fronted building; Trevor parked the buggy in one of the visitors' bays.

"Before we go in, don't you think it would be better if I went on my own?" I suggested.

"No," he said. "You don't know how things work here."

"Trevor, I'm asking about a friend, not running for office. I just thought that if I could talk to one of the nurses, explain why I was here, it might help." He thought about it for a second. Please say yes, I thought. I didn't want him getting in the way if I could help it.

"I'll bet you want Cy with you," he said at last.

"Perhaps she trusts me not to shaft her."

That was it, Trevor puffed out his chest. "Do you want to get out and talk about it?" he said. In answer, Cy opened his door and got out. He walked around to Trevor's side, stood by the door with his arms folded. Despite his offer Trevor didn't move, maybe his door had stuck? I sensed trouble. And we had only just got here. I jumped out and went to stand between Cy and the door.

"Boys," I said, "it won't look good, fighting in the car park and then asking them for help. Knock it off."

Cy looked annoyed. "He suggested it. Let's see what he's got; if he gets out." His tone suggested that he wasn't expecting it.

"Leave it, Cy. It's obvious that you don't get on but you can do that later. He's paying but I would have preferred to try things my way."

He nodded and stepped back, I tried to open Trevor's door, it was locked. There was a click; Trevor must have unlocked it because it opened the second time. Cy sneered at him as he climbed out. "One day soon," he said, just loud enough for Trevor to hear.

"What's the point of getting me out here if you're going to stand over me," I asked. "Are you frightened that I won't share?"

He didn't answer. "Or is there something that you're not telling me?" Again there was no reply; he just kept staring at Cy. Maybe he hadn't really noticed before. Cy had been to the gym on the station a lot and had toned up since he had been in London. Trevor was bigger but looked flabby. We couldn't carry on like this.

"Right, you two." I was going to put my foot down with a firm hand, or something. "I get it that you don't like each other, I don't like you much, Trevor, but you can both stop splashing your testosterone around until we figure out what's going on. If that's too much for you, well I'm off and you can grapple in the mud for all I care." I was shaking, had I pushed it too far?

Trevor looked surprised. "Where did that come from? OK, I'll calm down as long as he does."

"Cy," I said, "are you going to play nice?"

He nodded. "For you and for Maisie, but not for him. And if I find out he's..." They moved towards each other again and I stood between them.

"One more and I'm off," I warned. It was silent for a while.

"Come on then," Trevor said and the three of us went inside.

The place was spotless and white coated nurses bustled. There were pot plants and a lot of pictures on the walls. The guests, or clients or whatever, sat around watching video screens or talking, a few had earphones in and nodded to music. They all looked happy and well fed. A couple of them were walking up and down, aided by uniformed people who I took to be nurses or physiotherapists. The place had a restful, contented feel to it.

I led the three of us up to the desk. "How can I help you?" asked the girl without looking up from her screen. She was bent forward, concentrating, her fingers pattered on a keyboard. All I could see was her uniform cap with a few wisps of hair escaping from it. On the wall behind her was a gallery of smiling faces, under the heading 'Our Staff'.

"Hi, we've come to see…" Oh crap; who had we come to see? The fingers stopped and hovered.

"Kim Chok," supplied Trevor.

"Him." I added, "Please."

"Are you family?" she asked, still not looking up.

How was I going to get in to see him? It would have been easier without Trevor hanging around. I could actually operate better without him breathing down my neck. Perhaps I should have insisted, instead of just suggesting.

"No," I began, that made her look up at us.

"Well you can't see him, family only. And," she looked straight at Trevor, "you know that. I've told you already, twice."

"I'm sorry," I said, in pleading mode, we definitely should have left Trevor outside. "My friend Maisie looked after him and I need to ask him about something he told her." Her hand went to her face and she looked shocked.

"Oh, you're Maisie's friend," she said. "Are you the one she talked about all the time, Andrea or someone?"

"That's me, I'm Andi." Did she really talk about me all the time?

She got up and came round the desk, she gave me a hug. "You poor thing, it was awful and we had no idea she felt so bad." Her face fell. "She said you had fallen out and it was the worst day of her life. She missed you and was thinking of getting in touch to try and sort things out, she was just plucking up the courage. She knew where you were and all the excitement you'd been having. But I'm afraid I've got more bad news. I'm not supposed to give out the information but as you were a friend of Maisie's it'll be OK. I'm afraid that Mr Chok died three days ago."

Behind me I heard Trevor gasp. "Then we're too late," he muttered. Not "oh dear that's awful" just "we're too late." That was another thing for my list. What were we too late for?

Cy punched him on the arm. "Respect," he muttered.

The nurse continued, "I'm really sorry, I know how close Maisie and Kim had got, he told her all about his life and I know that she was interested."

"What did he used to do?" I asked.

"He was a journalist," she answered. "All the juicy gossip of the rich and famous."

"He told her something, the day before," Trevor said. "Is there any record of what he might have said, I don't know, cameras in the rooms, his papers anything like that."

She looked annoyed. "Am I repeating myself for the sake of it, you've been here before, several times, and been told the same thing. You're not a relative and I can't tell you. Now you," she pointed at me, "have a lot more reason to know, but the answer is still the same. We don't spy on our guests and any personal effects of Mr Chok will be released only to the persons named in his will. I have to get back to work." She walked back around the desk and sat.

So Trevor had come in and wound everyone up, maybe a bit of humility would have helped him. Would he learn? Probably not. I might have been able to talk to the nurse on my own. But his reappearance after he had upset people was plain daft.

There seemed little point in staying any longer, not here in the nursing home or on Mars in general, Trevor was going to have to think of another way to investigate. Or just accept it and move on. Strangely, despite my anger at his inept way of talking to people I felt better than I had in a long time. Maisie had been sorry and had wanted to mend our relationship. Pity it hadn't rubbed off on Trevor.

"Thank you," I said to the nurse. "I'm sorry to have bothered you."

She smiled. "That's OK, we were all devastated."

We went back towards the door. "I reckon you can take us back to get our things and then we can go to the port," said Cy. "Book the first tickets off this rock."

"We haven't finished yet," Trevor told him. "We have the police to see next."

"Have you managed to piss them off as well?" Cy asked. Oh great, they were starting again. He wasn't going to give up, that much was obvious and I suppose I had to respect him for that. But there was a problem with his attitude and the festering animosity with Cy. Trevor was going to reply but thought better of it.

As we got to the door, it opened to admit three large, dark suited men. They looked like undertakers; the taxi driver had said it was the trade to get into. It must be a big employer on Mars, what with all the old folk. They nodded politely to us, with the blank faces that undertakers all have and held the door for us to leave.

Trevor was agitated on the way to the police station; he kept looking in the rear-view mirror, as if he was checking that we weren't being followed. I asked him a few questions but he was distracted, at least he seemed to have got the hang of merging in with the traffic this time. I figured that the news of Kim's death had shaken him, that and his near fight with Cy. What he had hoped to get from Kim was anyone's guess now, what had he told Maisie that was so important?

Chapter 7

We pulled up outside the police station, it was dilapidated and crowded, a typical run-down municipal building. In contrast to the care home, this reception area was more like a war zone. People shouted and shoved, it smelt of sweat and last night's dinner.

After a crush and a wait, we were shown in to see a detective called Mayner; he sat behind a desk piled with papers and half-eaten sandwiches. Paper coffee cups were lined up. The place looked overworked and understaffed, the phones rang constantly and people hurried about. Was Mars a hotbed of crime, maybe they had gangs of mobility scooters joyriding on the pavements at six miles per hour or ram-raiding the shops?

"What can I do for you, Ms Pett?" he asked. "Mr Curtis has already been here several times, what's your connection to Ms Duncan?" I had to think for a second who Ms Duncan was; she had always been Maisie to me.

"Maisie was my best friend," I told him. "We grew up together and when Trevor, Mr Curtis, told me what had happened, it just seemed so out of character that I found it hard to believe."

"I understand," he said. "But it's not unknown here, people react differently to the situation, to the alien environment and way of life, it makes them do strange things."

"But to take an overdose and just lay down against a rock, it just doesn't feel right." I thought it was a good idea not to mention what I knew. That she had been told she would be very rich. Best not to muddy the waters just yet.

"I know and I'm sorry for your loss but I can assure you that we investigated properly, there was nothing to suggest that it was any more than that. Wait a minute," he said. "Ms Pett... aren't you the lady from the mining station out at Saturn?"

Here it comes, I thought, my reputation was about to bite my arse. I'd had all the fame and media attention I could handle after the Davina episode, my name and mugshot must have been seen in most places in the solar system.

"That's nothing to do with this," I tried to sound sincere. "Maisie was a friend of mine from way back, we were at school together. I've known Mr Curtis, Trevor, for a while too, the four of us worked together on Earth. When he told me what had happened I wanted to come and see for myself."

That was stretching the truth a bit but it sounded better than, 'he was shagging us both and I want to know if he killed her.'

"It's just out of character," said Cy, who had been looking uncomfortable in the surroundings.

"And you are?"

"I'm Ms Petts' business partner." Mayner nodded, as if he had heard of Cy as well. He ought to have, we had been interviewed together.

"When your name came up at arrivals, Andorra Pett, the crime-fighting Scooper pilot, I wondered if you were here to investigate something."

Oh great, I had been tracked from the start. I wasn't becoming the solar system's answer to Miss Marple for anyone. Mind you, crime-fighting Scooper pilot sounded pretty cool! I reckon I could pull that off.

"We didn't know about your connection to Mr Curtis," Mayner continued. Why hadn't Trevor told them? Another question; I needed a bigger brain to store them all.

"As I'm sure Mr Curtis has told you, there was no note found with her and nothing at her apartment or in her belongings. Her colleagues all said she was acting normally." He paused for a moment. "And we have no suspicious activity on the planet that we can associate with the events of that day." The way he said that wasn't quite right, as if it was forced somehow."

"And that makes you think it was suicide?"

He got up and crossed to a filing cabinet. "I don't have to show you this," he said, "but I'm going to. Mr Curtis has already seen parts of it. You've come a long way about a friend so I'll let you have a look. This is the report of our investigation. As you can see, we were thorough."

It was a thick folder and Cy and I bent heads and read it together. There was an introduction with personal details of Maisie, together with a photo that I remembered. Then a post mortem report, cause of death was listed as hypoxia resulting from depletion of pressure suit contents.

"Where's the bit about the pills?" I asked. Mayner pointed to the bottom of the sheet. Additional causes were a trace of zopiclone probably resulting in unconsciousness before death.

"What's zopiclone?"

"It's a sleeping pill," Trevor blurted. "I had them, she must have taken one." He had been quiet since we had walked into the police station, now he was sobbing. "If only I had kept them out of her way."

"If it's any comfort," Mayner said, "she would have been asleep long before she suffocated."

But why would she take them at lunchtime, just before she was going to work? Unless it really was a suicide. But then we were back to Kim Chok and why.

The next page was the log sheet from the emergency phone operator, it was more like a list, with times and comments in columns.

    14:10:05 Police operator, how can I help you?
    14:10:11 My partner, Maisie Duncan, has disappeared, she went off to work and she hasn't arrived. I've tried her cell phone and it just goes to voicemail.
    14:10:20 I see, sir, can you tell me your name, where she was going and when she left you.

14:10:26 I'm Trevor Curtis; she was going to The Murcheson care home in Eastown. She was due to start work at fourteen hundred. I got a call, I'm at work, Douglas Software.
14:10:41 And can you tell me her cell number please.
14:10:47 Err... (pause) 615-2783.
14:10:52 Thank you, sir, please stay where you are and don't try to call her again, we will locate her cell and update you.

There was something strange in that; it all seemed a bit hasty.

"Can I ask you, Detective, how come you investigated straight away; on Earth you'd leave it a while wouldn't you?"

He smiled. "Yes, but on Earth you can survive outside. On Mars, without a suit you have thirty seconds of agony. With a suit you have as long as you have oxygen, up to a couple of hours. That's assuming your suit doesn't spring a leak or you have some other accident, then you're back to the thirty seconds. We investigate straight away because we have to. Both the big airlocks have crews on standby, at a minute's notice to go out."

Hence the slipping out of an unmanned one then, this was looking more and more like it might just be suicide.

The next page was a copy from the police incident log, handwritten in bold ink. In among the other business of the desk, the relevant passage was highlighted in yellow.

14:12:00 Trace run on cell 615-2783, last tag location Airlock 3 Transponder recorded in motion outside airlock 11:55:37. Signal lost 12:01:13.
14:12:55 Airlock 3 contacted; operator reports one outward movement at 11:55:01 Licence ID Duncan. M. 375. Destination, sightseeing trip, one POB.
14:15:00 One SAR unit dispatched from Airlock 1, instructed to home on locator 615-2783.

I turned the page; Cy's breath was loud in my ear. **The next page was the radio log from unit Juliet Echo.**

14:15:05   Control, Juliet Echo, depressurising on SAR.
14:15:20   Control, Juliet Echo, we have acquired the cell signal approx. nine kilometres from our location, in the vicinity of Hecate. Requesting permission to proceed.
14:15:45   Control, roger, proceed, Juliet Echo, advise your progress.

There was a gap of several minutes in the timestamp.

14:22:47   Control, this is Juliet Echo, we are three hundred metres from the locator and have a vehicle, stand by.
14:22:52   Control, roger.
14:23:55   Control, Juliet Echo, vehicle is empty, no mechanical defects, proceeding to locator.
14:24:01   Control, roger.
14:24:35   Control, Juliet Echo, we have source, suited figure, they're sitting against a rock.
14:24:40   Control, roger.
14:26:15   Control, Juliet Echo, subject is female and deceased, suit air exhausted. Request backup, non-urgent.
14:27:00   Control, roger stand by in position.

That was it, in bold computer printout, non-urgent, it was too late to do anything but clear up.

I turned the page; there were a lot of pictures of the vehicle and of the suited figure sitting against the rock. She looked like she was on holiday; sat on the beach, staring out to sea.

My eyes welled up at the sight, even though the faceplate was opaque and you couldn't tell it was her, the knowledge that it was made it almost impossible to take in.

I hadn't noticed but Mayner had organised tea and now he gently took the file and passed the cups around.

"Do you want to read the rest?" he asked. "Or would you rather I gave you a summary."

I couldn't look at the rest; beside me Cy was silent, lost in thought.

"Just tell me," I said, "and what's a POB?"

"Person on board, don't you have them on your Scoopers?"

I shook my head. "No we're always alone, unless it's training then the Scooper ID is different."

"I understand. Of course we investigated, the vehicle was rented from a company on Main Street, it's the only place you can hire one. The owner said that it was all a very matter-of-fact transaction. Apparently Ms Duncan had rented from them several times before. She claimed to be fully qualified to go outside and stay for extended periods, we checked and she was; so no surprises there. The scene was searched for other people or vehicles but the terrain is rocky and there was no evidence, also there was a light breeze, some minor dust storm activity so there were no footprints or tracks we could trace, as far as we know she was alone."

Hang on a moment, I thought, when had Maisie learned to drive a Rover and got herself qualified? She hadn't driven a car on Earth; she reckoned living in London you didn't need to. And she was a city girl, loved the built-up vista, she even got agoraphobia in the park, what was going on?

"And that was it. The body was taken to our hospital and a post mortem performed. Nothing suspicious was found; just the presence of sleeping pills, which had been prescribed for Mr Curtis. Death was confirmed to be due to a lack of oxygen. We spoke to her solicitor and released her body to them, as her executors."

I was about to ask him about one of several things that didn't ring true about that when a uniformed policeman came into the room. "Cal," he said, "we have a lead on the POI from Earth."

Mayner looked annoyed, maybe we weren't meant to hear that, what was a POI anyway? Was it the same sort of thing as a POB?

"Excuse me," he said, standing. "If you need anything more, please get in touch but I have to leave you now. As far as we are concerned the investigation is over; as I said, I'm sorry for your loss."

He grabbed his jacket and followed the uniform out.

It all seemed very thorough, but I had a whole stack of questions. Why was she going outside, how long had she been going outside, why the sleeping pills and why hadn't Trevor mentioned any of the above? And what had made her want to learn to drive on Mars, where there was no need for it in the city. They would do for a start. And not a stupid question among them, I was getting good at this. We left the office, passed through the mayhem and were out on the street,

"Right," I said to Trevor as we sat in his buggy. "I want some information."

"You lied to us," said Cy.

Trevor hedged. "I never lied; everything that I told you was true."

"Don't be a prat! You might have told us some of the truth but not all of it. Why was she really going outside?"

"She wanted to explore, she was interested in going to this ridge place, she had time on her hands."

"That didn't sound like her; she was a city girl, she hated the wide open spaces. Why didn't you say you'd already upset the care home people?" He went red and I thought he was going to ask me to step outside. I'd have gone too.

"Bloody hell, Andi; is this how you treat your customers in that café of yours? I'm not on trial here."

"It stinks," Cy added. "Your behaviour, the whole thing, it just doesn't add up."

I had another go. "You wanted me to come and help, I need to know. Why were you on sleeping pills?"

He just looked at me. "That's bloody obvious isn't it, I couldn't sleep."

OK so that one *was* stupid.

We were getting nowhere, Trevor was getting more and more defensive and we were on the attack. We both sensed that there was a lot more to the story, the question was, how could we get him to admit it?

"Was she buried or cremated?" I asked him, trying to change the subject and calm things down a little.

"Cremated," he said. "There's a plaque in the garden of remembrance."

"Nice touch, Trevor," I said. "That was good of you."

"I had nothing to do with the plaque, I think the home organised it." Why had he said that? It made no sense. He might have been too upset to do much but surely he'd seen the will.

The will, that was another thing I wanted to see, it might give some insight. I'd have to find out about her solicitors, why did Trevor not know about it? Even if he wasn't a beneficiary it shouldn't have been a mystery to him. That was another question.

"I want to see where the plaque is."

"After lunch," Cy added, "somewhere nice."

"I've only got today off," Trevor said. "I have to go to work tomorrow, we have a lot on."

Thank goodness for that, I thought, we can get on without you cluttering the place up. Maybe I could sneak back to the care home without him.

We had a rather good lunch; the equivalent place to Derek's farm on Mars did as good a job as he did with the produce. Derek had told me that he knew the boss, Martin Squire; they had worked on an OLC platform years ago. "If you get a chance, say hello," he had told me. That reminded me, I must call Derek, let him know I was OK.

The food was pricey but that didn't bother us, it certainly didn't seem to bother Trevor. "Have what you want," he said.

"Can I see the will?" I asked. He hedged.

"I don't know where it is, I haven't seen it myself, there's a whole load of her stuff at the apartment. The police took it apart looking for a note. I haven't been able to face sorting it all out. You can come and help yourself." You would think that he would want to find it, unless he had and wasn't in it.

We left the restaurant and drove through the manic traffic to the garden of remembrance, it was in a side tunnel and was a tranquil place, in a much bigger cave, laid out with soil and trees and grass. There were graves as well as the plaques and a gardener tending and watering a whole array of roses. Trevor took us to a wall, festooned with plaques, together with the graves there were a lot of dead people on Mars, considering how short its time as an outpost of humanity had been.

Maisie's was a simple metal plate, on a wooden background with a border of flowers. 'Maisie Duncan' it said with her birthday and a Martian date that meant little to me. There was no other comment, no 'rest in peace' or 'ever loved' or anything like that. And whoever had engraved the plaque had made a mistake; her birthday was in October, not January: 10 not 01. I said nothing, but it was another strange thing to add to the list.

I said a few things to Maisie in my head as we stood silently, faced by the finality that the plaque represented. I realised that life was too short and unpredictable to hold a grudge. That death was so much more final than worrying about a shag. I said I was sorry that I had never tried to get in touch, sorry that I had hated her instead of trying to understand. I wondered what Trevor was thinking, Cy too. They both stood, deep in thought.

We didn't speak, after a few minutes I left them and walked back towards Trevor's buggy. There was a tousle-haired boy of about ten standing by it. I figured he was after something, money probably. I was just about to tell him to get lost when I realised that I had seen him before, outside the hotel.

"Are you Andi?" he said.

"Who the hell are you?"

"I'm Murph, are you Andi or not?"

"Why?"

"Cos! I gotta message for Andi, from Maisie. I was at the hotel this morning but I couldn't get you on your own."

This was interesting. Trevor and Cy were out of earshot. Good. "Yes I'm Andi," I said.

"What was your shop called on Earth?"

"AC Couture." He nodded and pressed an envelope into my hands. "She said to keep it from him," he said and ran off before I could ask him how he knew I was coming.

As he ran down the tunnel a suited man came into view, he tried to grab Murph but he dodged past him. It was a long way away but he looked like one of the three we had seen at the home.

I slipped the envelope into my pocket as Trevor and Cy came up to me. "What did he want?" asked Trevor.

"Just money, I told him to get lost."

"Lucky he didn't knife you," he said. "He must have seen me coming."

I was quite happy to let Trevor believe he was my saviour if it distracted him. Cy was stood behind Trevor miming putting his fingers down his throat and gagging. He said nothing but then he spotted the suit as well, he was looking at him over my shoulder. We got into the buggy. As we drove past him and rounded a bend in the tunnel I could see where the other two suits had got to, they had hold of Murph and were shaking him.

"Weren't they at the care home?" I said to Trevor, as we passed them and rejoined the main road.

"Who?" he answered.

"Those blokes in the suits back there, shaking the boy."

Trevor looked around, his expression changed twice, first to worry, then to that fixed grin he did when he was lying. "Oh them, they look like undertakers to me, no surprise there then; undertakers at a care home and again at a crematorium. Maybe the boy was trying to rob them; you said he was after money. Andi, there's no conspiracy here, we're not being followed. It's a small place, you see the same people every day, especially if you've been here a while."

That was probably true; it certainly was on the station. And the cab driver had said it too. Maybe I was just imagining it but it felt to me like we were being followed by them. They had that shifty look and Trevor had been agitated each time, no matter what he said.

Surely he was protesting too much, I'd never suggested that there was a conspiracy. And if they were just innocent undertakers, why had they grabbed the boy who had delivered the envelope?

"I'll drop you at the hotel and come back for dinner," Trevor said. "I have to go and make some calls, I've been away too long and I'm back in the office tomorrow. We can have a proper talk this evening over a meal and a drink and decide what to do next." I couldn't think of anything other than what was in my pocket. Hopefully I could have a read before dinner, maybe it would explain everything.

"Don't put yourself out too much," said Cy. "I'd hate to keep you from your oh so important work, especially after you got us all the way here to help you." Trevor went red and his hands gripped the wheel tightly. He said nothing.

The rest of the journey back passed in silence. Trevor dropped us at the hotel and drove off, without a goodbye. I grabbed Cy and spun him to face me.

"Calm down, will you," I said. "I know you want to fight him, can't you wait till we've done what we came here for. Maisie's still dead and I have to cope with that and your antics, it's too much." I started to cry, it wasn't an exaggeration, dealing with what I had heard and seen today and keeping them apart were two separate jobs and I felt like I only had the strength for one.

It had been all very well, spending Trevor's money and winding him up on the journey, now I was here and the reality of it all was facing me I felt exhausted. Seeing the police report with its pictures and the bold facts had brought it home to me, then the plaque on the wall made it even worse. And the envelope was burning a hole. But although Cy wanted to deal with Trevor he had to be patient, surely he could see that I was entitled to a bit of grief.

He hugged me. "I'm sorry, Andi, I'll go easy on him. We're all pretty emotional right now and today's had enough excitement. But can I wind him up a little, like he used to do to me all the time, please?"

I smiled. "Just a little wouldn't hurt, enough to keep him on his toes."

Back in my hotel room, I held the envelope in my hands. Should I get Cy in before I opened it? I didn't know who the 'he' was that Murph had said shouldn't see it. Probably Trevor but you couldn't be too careful. I opened it, I could always tell Cy later.

Inside were two sheets of paper and a memory card in its plastic case. Not another memory card, I'd seen enough of them on the station; at least the letter wasn't in code. I unfolded them and started to read, recognising the handwriting immediately.

Chapter 8

Andi, I don't know where to begin, the letter began. *I'm probably the last person you want to have anything to do with but you're the only one I can think of that can help me. I know that I don't deserve it for the way I've behaved. I realise that, but I've found something so important that I can't trust it to anyone else. Especially not to Trevor; and you'll soon see why.*

I took a deep breath, it wasn't suicide then, Trevor was involved in it, no matter what he said.

What Trevor and I did in London was wrong, but when he made his move he said that you and he were over and I honestly believed him. After I tell you what's happened to me since that day you'll realise that it could have been you in the position that I'm in, you had a lucky escape and if you're reading this then I've paid the price.

Oh, you poor thing, I thought. Hang on a minute, you're a lying turd Trevor, unless you were really going to end it. I certainly hadn't been planning it; back then I had thought that Trevor was the one. I read on.

We had to leave Earth because Trevor got involved with some very dubious people, he thinks I don't know about his gambling and his money problems, the way he chose to get out of it was so wrong it was almost stupid. He sold the shop and everything in it to pay off one lot of trouble and fund a new start here.

I shook my head in disbelief, he'd done what? Flogged my business and my house to pay his debts! OK so I shouldn't have just walked away like that and maybe I could have checked into the state of things from time to time but I hadn't. If I'd have known he would do that I wouldn't have been so honest and only taken my share of the money from our accounts. There were five years of my sweat in there, the house that my parents had left me and my sister. I had thought that I would have got something back. My hands were shaking as I read on.

We moved here to get away and start over. But what does he do as soon as we got here but go straight back to his old ways, playing cards and borrowing money. And he's so dumb that he goes straight back to the same gang of loan sharks. Things went wrong and he couldn't keep up the payments, then he lost his job because he was too busy trying to keep them off his back to do any actual work.

We had to live off my wages while he found something else to do, he reckons he's retrained in software programming. I never really found out what he did but I think that he works for the gang now. He's being threatened to pay back the money he's borrowed but hasn't got. And if he finds out what I know, it'll all be gone for nothing when it shouldn't be.

I've been looking after a man at the care home – Kim Chok. He has a secret and no-one except me to share it with. And I've helped him; I've eased his pain and just been nice to him.

He used to be a journalist and the other page is a copy from one of his old notebooks. Somehow, and I don't know all the details, he found a load of stolen property and smuggled it onto Mars to fund his retirement. He used to go out with his wife and bring back small amounts of it every now and then, so as not to make it too obvious. What's left is still hidden and he wants me to have it. I've been getting myself organised to go and retrieve it, I've learnt to drive a Rover and got qualified in my days off. I've told Trevor it's for a holiday plan but I'm not sure if he believes me. I've even managed to get out with Kim a few times and he's shown me where the loot is hidden. But now he's too ill to go out any more.

This just got more and more involved, why couldn't it have just been suicide, with this being a note that said it had all got too much for her. But then it explained the suits, they must be the bad guys. And Trevor knew that, hence the agitation.

Trouble is, some of the people it belonged to on Earth have got wind of it and they're here looking for it. And they're friends with the ones that Trevor is in debt to.

If I let on, Trevor gets the money and uses it to pay off his debts. There's more than enough for that. But they seem to know how much there should be and I reckon that if we admit to having it they'll kill him and me for the rest. And Kim's spent some of it, so there's not as much as they're expecting.

I'd reached the end of the page and stopped reading, my tears were welling up. Oh Maisie, what had you got yourself into? And she was right, if I had still been with Trevor it could have been my name on that plaque. How I wished she hadn't fallen for him, or had been brave enough to walk out like I had.

Cy rattled on the door. "Oy Andi, I'm going down for dinner, I shouldn't say it but it's another chance to fleece Trevor's expenses. I'm really sorry about earlier, you coming?"

I jammed the papers back in the envelope and stuffed it into my pocket. I would have to pretend that I hadn't seen it until I had read the rest; that could be tricky with Cy to say the least. I wasn't renowned for my poker face at the best of times. And Trevor would be turning up as well, how could I face him knowing what I did?

"Just coming," I called, trying not to sound like I'd been crying. By the time I had dried my eyes and made myself presentable he had got fed up with waiting and was nowhere to be seen. Pig, I thought and followed him down to the restaurant.

Sure enough Cy was on my case straight away; he already had a beer and a plate of appetisers; well, half a plate to be exact.

"Trevor never spotted that then did he?" he remarked as I sat down and picked up the menu.

"What?" I tried, no dice.

"C'mon, Andi, this is me. I can read you like a bloody book, so can anyone. I saw the boy pass you something." He reached over and held my hand, tenderly for a big bloke. "And you've been grizzling again, what's going on, love? Is it Maisie or me and Trevor?" He was a sentimental fool sometimes but he did care about me, all I ever did was drag him into my dramas. He was only getting at Trevor to protect me.

I took a deep breath. "This is serious, Cy," I said. "Maisie left me a letter and somehow that boy at the garden of remembrance had it. He was the same boy that I saw here this morning. She must have known things were getting bad and that I would come. I've only looked at a bit of it but I think I know why Maisie ended up where she did."

He nodded. "I knew it, I bloody well knew it." The concerned expression vanished, replaced by anger. He clenched his fists, the muscles in his forearms bunched. "And the suits had the boy; didn't they?"

"Yes, did you notice that Trevor was agitated both times we saw them?"

He ate a weird looking concoction. "Yeah, I saw that. These are good, no idea what they're made out of but they're good," he said. "You should have one, take your mind off things."

"Pay attention, Cy, stop thinking about your stomach for five minutes."

"Sorry," he said. "I'm being insensitive, what else?"

"For another thing, it wasn't suicide. From what I've read it was almost definitely murder, or at the very least an accident. But it was made to look like suicide."

He didn't look as shocked as I had expected. "And what about his lordship's part in it, I never liked him and I can tell from the way he's been behaving that he's got more to do with this than he lets on. Was it him?"

"You're right there as well," I agreed. "He's up to his neck in it, no matter what he says, but I don't think he killed her himself."

"Before you told me about the letter I'd have thought it was suicide," he said. "All we heard today seemed to confirm it. Tell me what the letter says."

I wasn't about to start that though, I might have to stop halfway.

"Later. Trevor will be here in a moment, it's better if you don't know what's in it before you see him. Somehow, I've got to keep a straight face; both of us would never manage it. When he turns up, let's just go with suicide, I'll suggest there's no reason for us to stay and watch his reaction. And try to stay calm."

Cy grinned. "OK, after all, he wanted you to come and see what you thought. If that was genuine, now you've done that we can go back home. By the way, you look bloody awful."

"Thanks, Cy, perhaps it'll hide my giveaway expression."

"If he even notices."

I reckoned that my plan was logical and very devious. We might learn a lot from his reaction.

We ordered some more appetizers and I got a glass of wine, in fact I got the bottle, in a metal ice bucket. Cy had another beer.

Trevor arrived and we both switched into bland mode and exchanged greetings.

"Hi." He was cheerful. "Sorry I had to dash off, I've been away longer than I said and my boss is demanding. I've got a mountain of work tomorrow and I'll be in the office late every day for a week. What are we having? It's all good."

Was this a new attempt at friendship from him? Maybe he had thought better of provoking Cy. Maybe my threat to leave had bothered him.

We both plumped for the most expensive things we could stomach, along with another bottle of wine. He hadn't noticed my face, blotched from crying. I was going to say that the day had upset me, if he bothered to ask. If I could cry it might hide my real knowledge that Cy was right, he needed a good dose of retribution for what he had done to my friend.

Trevor was in a good mood; he was as charming as I remembered he could be, back in the days when we were happy together. He soon spotted my distressed expression and apologised again. He tried to be consoling and sympathetic. What a change from his stroppy act earlier! Something since he dropped us off must have cheered him up.

Over an excellent meal we actually had a civilised discussion about our lives, almost as if the thing that set us on this path had never had the effect that it did. Cy kept his temper in check and it was almost a pleasant evening. When he wanted, Trevor could be good company, the wine and beer might have helped relax everyone.

"When she heard about what you did on the station," Trevor said, "both of you, the way you sorted things out and caught that killer, she was so impressed. 'That's my Andi' she said, 'if ever you need some help, she's the one'."

Now it was his turn to look sad and for a moment I could almost think that the letter was the lie, he could have been a politician, he was on sincerity overload.

"What have you been up to here then?" Cy asked as the conversation faltered.

"Oh, I've been busy," he replied. "I got fed up with accountancy and retrained in software programming. There was a lot more money in it." That fitted with the letter but wasn't the truth. It was just another lie. How much of his good mood was a lie as well?

In the end we ran out of things to say about Mars and his life; the subject turned to our thoughts on what we had learned about Maisie. I said that based on what I had seen and heard I thought that suicide was the most likely verdict.

"So do I," said Cy. Trevor looked annoyed.

"Why? I thought you'd think it was funny."

"What's funny? She took your pills, found a way to go outside without detection and did the deed."

"Yeah but she left her locator on so we could find her."

"Perhaps she forgot. Perhaps she wanted you to rescue her," suggested Cy. "They reckon that most suicides are a cry for help that goes unanswered. Maybe she was giving you a chance to prove yourself by saving her." That was more devious behaviour from him.

Trevor looked annoyed, not sad or upset, Cy was making him feel guilty and so he should be, especially given what I knew. He might not have killed her but the way she said he was living can't have made her life a bed of roses.

I gave him my decision. "It was a waste of time dragging us here, Trevor, we might as well go home. Maisie killed herself, we'll never know why but it's done now. There's nothing to keep us here."

Trevor looked panicked. "You can't go," he said. "You haven't gone through her things for clues yet or seen her solicitor or anything." His eyes were wide in desperation and his voice was raised. I could see people on the adjoining tables were starting to take notice. I looked around and spotted one of the three suits over in the corner. I know even undertakers had to eat but this was getting creepy. It was definitely him; he was one of the two who had been holding the boy, Murph.

As my eye passed over him he ducked his head and concentrated on his food, my eye carried on and I saw a video screen in the corner. It was showing a news channel with the sound turned off, the building on the screen looked familiar. I nudged Cy. "Look at that."

He glanced up. "Isn't that the care home we were at? It looks like they've been robbed."

The lower-third of the screen had a rolling ticker, it appeared that all the guest rooms had been burgled by a gang who had pretended to be undertakers to get inside, then had locked the building down and ransacked the place. I had the sudden feeling that they were looking for the thing that I had in my pocket.

"All those places look the same," Trevor said, turning his head. "There's hundreds of care homes here and everyone knows there's valuables in them. It must be a coincidence."

"Like us seeing the same people everywhere we went?"

He didn't answer that, instead he returned to his plea. "Can you do a bit more digging; please, at least you could see the solicitor tomorrow? The next shuttle isn't for a few days so you're here till then anyway."

"We might as well do a bit of shopping while we're here." I grudgingly offered, "I suppose we could do a bit of asking around while we're about it, if that'll make you happy."

His relief was palpable. "Thank you. Like I said, I have to go back to work so I can't take you places."

"That's OK we can manage. If I can get an appointment I'll see Maisie's solicitor. Who was it?"

He looked at his watch. "I can't remember, it's in her papers I guess, I'll let you know, drop it off in the morning." He suddenly seemed eager to get away. "I gotta go," he announced. "I have to make a call." It was nine pm, it seemed a little late for calls but then, he didn't say what it was about. It was OK, I wanted him gone anyway; we had things to discuss.

"Goodnight," we said in unison. He left and about ten seconds later the suit followed. Perhaps that explained his hasty departure; he must have seen him when he turned to look at the news.

"Good, he's gone," Cy was fuming. "I don't think I could have resisted the urge to thump him for much longer."

"Wait till you read Maisie's letter. What are we going to do tomorrow? We could snoop about, see the people who hired the Rover, the solicitors," I suggested.

Cy had a better idea. "Or we could have a day to ourselves, do some sightseeing and try to find out why we're being followed. We'll have a look at the letter in a moment, for now let's have some dessert, then I feel like cheese and biscuits."

We finished our meal, feeling as bloated as a pair of pythons and went back to my room. I wanted to see the rest of Maisie's letter and Cy needed to get up to speed. We settled in, him on the sofa, handy for the mini-bar and me in an armchair by the desk.

"OK, where is it?" he asked, grabbing a bottle of Scotch and opening it.

"Let me finish it while you get comfortable." I opened the envelope and pulled the pages back out, the memory card fell on the floor. Cy pounced on it. "Oh great, another one of these, have you done anything with it yet?"

"No," I said. "It's not mentioned in the letter so far. We can worry about that later."

I turned the letter over, there was only one paragraph that I hadn't read.

Chapter 9

The other page will tell you all you need to know to find the stash, I'm keeping quiet but Trevor may find out what I know and things might get difficult. Whatever you do, when you've got the stuff, and I know you'll get it cos you don't give up, promise me that you'll keep him and all the bad guys away from it.

She had scrawled: *Good luck, Luv ya, Maisie* and added kisses at the bottom, I handed it to Cy and looked at the other page as he read.

It was a photocopy of a notebook page, the writing neat. There was a list of map references and numbers. They must have been directions to a point across the crater. Then some distances and a drawing of a piece of landscape, a narrow crevice in cliffs. It had a distinctive shape, a single entrance that split into two inside. Underneath that was a sketch of a child's face, 'use your torch here' was written by the drawing. There was an arrow pointing down from below the chin.

Cy finished the letter and passed it back, his face was sombre. "How do you do it, Andi?" he asked, his voice cracking with emotion. "Is it some sort of gift you've acquired since you caught them at it and we left Earth?"

"What?" I said, handing him the other sheet.

"You only have to breathe out and you land us in trouble." He sounded exasperated and I could see his point.

I hadn't exactly had a quiet life since that day back in London. And yet it had started like any other.

Chapter 10

London, in late spring. Probably the best time of the year. The tulips were just starting to get replaced by the riot of hot summer colours, as it got warmer; dour winter clothes were also being replaced by the brighter clothes of the season. And there was the anticipation of lazy days in the sun. The city hadn't become the humid, unpleasant place it would be by August.

This year I was making a big effort with my clothes shop. I had spent five years building up a select clientele with my designs, offering mainly summer wear that tried to be different to the vast majority of offerings from the multiples and run-of-the-mill names. And this year was shaping up to be my best yet.

People had started buying my creations in midwinter for their holidays in the sun. My idea of a shop that only sold one season's clothes was vindicated, money was pouring in and I was happy. My two best friends were working for me and the love of my life was involved as well. What could possibly go wrong?

But for the first time I was about to get bitten on the arse by life. I had been seeing Trevor Curtis for nearly three of those five years. He was an accountant, that's how we'd met, when I needed my books doing he had been the junior assigned to sort my finances into something that wouldn't attract a fine, or peals of laughter, from the taxman.

He had sorted out my paperwork, then in the face of his handsome good looks I had let him attend to a few more of my needs, which resulted in his moving in to my flat, over the shop in the house that my parents had left me.

Back then, Cy was my cutter and tailor, he made all my designs into samples which we then outsourced to manufacture. Maisie, my lifelong friend, was my assistant and the person responsible for stock and keeping on top of things.

It worked like a dream. AC Couture was going places, magazines were starting to notice us and we had interviews and articles lined up to keep us in the public eye for the summer months.

That fateful afternoon, I had popped up to the flat for a cup of tea. The shop was quiet and I thought that it was just me and Cy in the building. He was working out in the back and there were no customers. I called through and he agreed that tea was a good idea. "And make sure you do more than wave the bag at the milky water," he warned; my tea was never strong enough for his liking. I grinned as I walked to the stairs.

"Five minutes," I called back. "And I'll bring biscuits."

So you can imagine my surprise when I got upstairs and heard noises coming from my bedroom. And it definitely wasn't burglars; I could tell what was going on straight away, the voices left little doubt as to what was required compared to what was being delivered. Burglars never shouted, "Harder! Faster!" at least not in Blackheath.

I blushed, my mum would have fainted. Then I got very angry, because I recognised both voices. I went to the kitchen for a weapon.

I managed to get the bedroom door open without disturbing the performance, I was hidden by a short corridor from the scene of the action anyway and holding my weapon of choice I crept toward the sound.

A bucket of water holds about nine litres; this one was filled from the cold tap and included ice cubes from the fridge and a little anti-bacterial solution – my attempt to clean up the language. I let them have the lot, followed by the empty plastic bucket, which bounced satisfyingly off a turned head. In those milliseconds the look on the two faces was, as they say, priceless.

"I can explain," said Trevor, retreating behind the bed, his appearance at that point suggested why his companion, my best bloody friend, had been shouting 'Harder'.

"Andi," she began, revealing that at least she hadn't been too far gone to remember whose bed she was in.

"Out," I said. "I'll be back in five minutes and it'll be bleach in the next bucket."

Then I went into the bathroom and cried as I heard their hasty departure.

About half an hour later I was still sat on the loo sobbing. It felt like my insides had been pulled out, slowly. There was a tentative knock on the door.

"Bugger off," I shouted.

"Andi," Cy's voice called. "Let me in, love."

"Leave me alone, Cy."

"Don't be such a drama queen, I've got you tea and choccie biscuits."

That was different. I got up, weak-kneed and opened the door.

Cy was smirking and trying to hide it, his eyebrows dancing over his forehead like two small furry animals.

"Well," he said theatrically. "Trevor wasn't such a big man after all then." He paused – a trick of his. "At least not when he flashed past me."

"Has he gone?"

He hugged me. "They both have. He had his trousers on inside out but hadn't zipped; it was like an elephant impersonation contest."

Despite the feeling of betrayal, by not one but two of my closest friends, I had to laugh.

Chapter 11

Cy's voice brought me back to the present. "We have to decide what we're going to do about all this," he said. "Things have changed, we started off coming to investigate Maisie's suicide, now we know," he waved the paper about, "that it wasn't. There's something out there and we have to get it."

"I don't want it, Cy. Maisie died for it and it's not worth it. I'm for leaving it there, pretending that we never got this letter and going home."

He shook his head. "OK maybe you don't want whatever it is but think of this. Maisie died to make sure that Trevor didn't get his hands on it and she asked you to make sure that he doesn't get it."

"We can do that, Cy. Just leave and take the knowledge with us."

"You're not thinking straight, you'll always know what you did. You'll wonder what you left, change your bloody mind and want to come back. Do you think that nobody will come after you? After they've gone to the trouble of getting you here, of paying for all this? There're some serious people involved. I don't see why Trevor should get it because we didn't bother to do what Maisie wanted and stop him. If we go, and you have to remember that there's no guarantee that we'll be able to, that's what'll happen. And it's not just about you, I'm in on it as well and I'm not so squeamish."

"What do you mean? Do you reckon that we can't leave?"

"Think about it, Trevor got us here, now we find that there's more to it. Trevor might not know what Murph gave us but he knows there's something. And so do the bad guys."

He was making sense. It was sobering to think that we might not be able to leave. And he was right; I owed it to Maisie to finish what she had started. I could always give the money to someone; a charity would be pleased with it. We had to stay.

He had finished looking at the notebook page and laid it down. His expression said it all. "I'm glad I didn't read any of that before we had dinner," he said. "I wouldn't have been able to sit down with him if I'd have known all that two hours ago. How did you not use your steak knife on him?"

"It wouldn't have brought her back," I said. "And now I've thought about it, I'm a new member of your 'I want to see him suffer and know there's no way out camp'."

He smiled. "Good. Here's what I think." He reached over the side of the sofa, pulled another bottle of Scotch from the mini-bar and took a swig straight from it; he had class, no doubt about that.

"Throw me one of those bottles," I suggested. "Any one of them will do." If I didn't keep up there would be none left for me. I copied him; opening and tipping. After all, glasses were for losers.

He cleared his throat and started, "First of all; I was right. Trevor is in it up to his eyeballs. All his 'she was going to tell me later and didn't' talk; that's obviously a load of bollocks."

I had to agree, this had been going on for a while. The fact that she had learnt to drive and conquered her fear of open spaces to go out with Kim proved that.

He carried on. "The bad guys tracked Kim down; they must have been on the trail of the stuff, perhaps he had changed his name, whatever. They found Kim, saw that he was being looked after by Maisie and they added it all up. Maybe they visited him, he let on that she was in on it."

That made sense so far. It was one of those sets of circumstances that shouldn't happen but always seemed to. "Go on then, Sherlock, you're getting good at this."

Cy finished the bottle, hardly difficult as there was only a mouthful in them, and threw it delicately towards the bin. It sank into the middle with a clunk.

"Two points," he said. "Right, where was I? Oh yeah, these bad guys, they didn't get the information out of the old bloke but they find out that Maisie and Trevor are an item. They decide to lean on Maisie; then they find out that Trevor is already being leant on. So they join forces with the other guys. When they realise that as well as the loans, they have the chance for extras; they must have thought it was Christmas. Trevor then put pressure on Maisie as well and when she didn't say where the stuff was, someone killed her."

Whew, that was some theory, but I had to admit it was plausible, except for one thing.

"Unless…" I said and Cy suddenly realised that it wouldn't make sense to kill her if she hadn't said anything.

"Unless she told them the wrong place and they killed her for that," he added.

There was another possibility though.

"Maybe they already have the stuff and they killed her so she couldn't tell," I suggested.

"Then why are they still here?"

"Perhaps they're deciding whether to kill Trevor?"

"I can help them with that," he declared with relish.

"We don't know how much stuff there was," I added. "Was it cash, jewellery, bonds, gold bars? It might need a lot of lifting or disguising and they're getting themselves organised."

Cy had clearly been thinking, through all the banter. "No, they wouldn't be following us if they knew where the stuff was, they wouldn't care. And Trevor wouldn't be desperate to get you here and to keep you here if they knew what we just found out. They'd be busy getting whatever it is off-world or legitimised somehow."

"How do you do that?"

He looked exasperated. "They're criminals, Andi. They launder money, buy things with stolen cash, change it into legal things. They *know* people who can do that."

I tried to get my mind around this new world, so if the bad guys were interested in us that must mean…

"Then Trevor has got us here to find out what he couldn't from Maisie."

Cy stopped inspecting the little shelf in the fridge that had packets of nuts and chocolate bars on it. "How do you mean?"

"Well, if Maisie never told them and they killed her, then the only way they can hope to get the stuff is if they think that she might have told me."

"Like she has?" he said. "Except they didn't know that."

And then with a jolt I thought of Murph.

"What about if that boy has let on?"

"The boy who gave you the envelope?"

"Yeah, as we drove away, remember, two of the suits had him; one of them was in the restaurant when we had dinner."

"That could explain why Trevor was happy." It could indeed.

"We need to use this information, this notebook page. All these directions and drawings of the cliffs. It must be outside the city, probably near the place where Maisie's vehicle had been found."

"So she might have been taking them out to retrieve it when she was killed. We need a proper map." He changed the subject. "I wonder what's on the memory card?"

"Dunno, it won't fit in my phone and I don't want to use the viewer in the room, just in case."

Cy looked concerned. "Do you think the room's bugged?"

"I think that we can't be too careful, maybe we've said too much already, perhaps we should only talk about it when we're out in the open."

He digested that. "You're probably right," he said after a while. "We'll need to get a portable reader."

"We can do that tomorrow as well."

"We can't let on to Trevor that we know any of this." That would be hard; at least he was going back to work and we wouldn't see as much of him.

"He might have got an idea, if the boy said anything."

"What did he know? That Maisie gave him an envelope for you.

He wouldn't know what was in it; it might just have been a letter saying sorry, it might have been the missing suicide note."

That was true; there was little we could do about it.

"So, if we do a few touristy things tomorrow and get the map and the reader it'll be a way of messing them about," said Cy. "Dragging them all over Tharsis while they think we're getting closer to the stuff, except that they won't know it's for nothing."

"There are a few other things we could do whilst we're here," I added, thinking of the awkward bit that I couldn't explain, even to myself. It had been nagging at me ever since I knew we were coming to Mars, now I had to get it out of my system.

"Here it comes," said Cy. "Spit it out; what other things?"

Chapter 12

"I've been wondering about Derek's wife, you remember that she came here?"

Cy gave me his best death stare. "I do not believe you, Andi."

"What? It's been on my mind all the time since Trevor wanted me to help. Derek didn't want to visit Davina in case he ran into her."

"I can understand that," he said. "But you've never met her, you wouldn't know her if you fell over her. You said you had enough to cope with, why do you want to rake all that up? Seriously, you should leave it all, Andi. You and Derek are good together, you start finding out about his ex-wife and her love-child and it'll do you no good."

He was right of course, I was just distracting myself with the notion.

"And," he waved his finger in the general direction of me, "you'll get no thanks. You're not even supposed to know about it. Do you think Derek will thank you, or her come to that? What do you intend to say? 'HI, I'm Andi, your husband's with me now, I know all about what you got up to. And I put your daughter in prison. Have you got a message for him?'."

Oh hell, there was that as well as the things that I wasn't supposed to know about. Cy pressed on.

"So what were you going to talk about?" he asked. "I take it you realise that if you start you will have to admit you found the book. Cos that's the only way you could know. Haven't we got enough else going on? Were you going to invite her for a meal, perhaps have tea?" His sarcasm knew no bounds.

"OK, OK, Cy, I give up, you're right."

"Yes I am, cos if you do that, everyone will hear about it and know that you've seen the book. You remember, that book we managed to convince the police had never existed. I think it's a mistake, getting involved in tracking her down, especially if you're serious about Derek." He got up. "And if that's the conversation you want to have now, I think I'll be off. Don't do it, keep well out of it, call Derek if you must but don't breathe a word, he won't want you to see her."

With that he walked out, the door slammed shut.

I was daft to even think about it, if I was honest, I only wanted to see Helen because people on the station had said that I looked like her. And if I did, was Derek only interested in me because of it? Should I call him and ask? And now I'd upset Cy.

I opened the fridge, there was a solitary bottle of gin left; it went down in one gulp.

Chapter 13

Next morning we had our breakfast and waited around for Trevor to come and give us the information about the solicitor. He never showed by nine; he must have forgotten. My head felt better, despite all the shocks of the day before. And I had thought about what I had said.

"You were right, Cy," I admitted, "about Derek's wife; it would be a stupid thing to do."

He smiled. "Sometimes you seem determined to snatch defeat from the jaws of victory, isn't there enough going on to keep you amused? Please tell me that you didn't call him last night."

"No I didn't, I just drank another bottle of gin and went to sleep."

"I'm relieved to hear it, now where's the cause of all our grief got to? Why don't you call him?"

As he said it; it dawned on me that I, we, couldn't.

"Do you know his number then, Cy, cos he never told me."

"Oh," he said as it occurred to us both that Trevor hadn't told us his number, or where he lived or anything. I felt slightly foolish. I went to the desk, they had no details, the bill was registered to Douglas Software and the desk had no numbers for Mr Curtis.

"Sod him then," said Cy when I told him. "We told him we were going shopping, let's just do that and keep racking up the expenses till he appears."

Cy and I set off from the hotel, a leisurely stroll into Main Street, the commercial centre of Tharsis. We stopped and looked in each shop we came to; it was a novelty after the spartan shopping conditions of the station. There were real things here; you actually had a visible choice, instead of just collecting stuff you'd ordered from a screen. Unlike most men, Cy was a pleasure to go shopping with. He was attentive and full of good schemes for the things I was interested in. And he spotted a few things that he wanted for himself.

There was some equipment that we could use in the café and I bought it and arranged for its delivery. It would be something to look forward to when we finally got back. And I was going back, I wasn't stopping here a minute longer than I needed to.

As a bonus, all the looking in big windows and wandering around being tourists was a good excuse to spot followers.

"I've clocked the three guys in dark suits," Cy said after a long period of window gazing. "They're spread out, so they can cover us whichever way we go without looking too obvious."

"I keep seeing the same two guys in casual gear," I replied. "They're almost falling over the suits."

"What, do you think that there are two lots following us?"

"Well Maisie did say that there were two gangs, the lot that Trevor owed and the lot that were chasing Kim, perhaps they're both watching us?"

Why, I wondered, couldn't my life be more normal? Even now, I wasn't able to grieve properly for my friend.

I had to find out that she might have been murdered, not content with that, I was now being followed around Mars by gangsters. And it seems that one gang wasn't enough, I had to have two lots of dubious types following me. Cy was right, I didn't need to pack any more problems in. Perhaps I should be more proactive, find out how serious they were.

"Let's see if we can lose them," I suggested, as we gazed at a selection of clothing in a shop situated on a corner, a small alleyway led away into darkness about two metres from us.

"Won't that give the game away?" he said. "If we disappear they'll know we're onto them."

"Not if we do it like dumb tourists, anyway what can they do? If they killed Maisie by mistake they're hardly likely to do it again. I'm sick of being manipulated, let's have a little fun."

"Why don't I like this idea?" said Cy. "You're crazy, Andi."

We ambled away from the window and turned quickly down the side of the building. I grabbed Cy and dragged him into the shadow of a doorway, before either group had chance to come around the corner. The building ended twenty metres past our hiding place, with a choice of left or right.

"Thought my luck was in," he gasped.

"Shh," I replied as I peered out from the doorway.

The first group appeared, it was the suits, all pretence of separation had been abandoned. When they couldn't see us, they ran down the alley in a tight bunch. We ducked back and they passed us, unseen in the deep shadow of the doorway. We looked back out again as the other two came into view. They watched the receding figures and stopped. One pulled out a cell phone; we were close enough to hear his side of the conversation.

"They ran off, Cal," he said. I had a memory, back at the police station, someone had called Detective Mayner 'Cal'. Maybe these two were police, perhaps they were watching the three suits and not us.

"I think the second lot are police," I said to Cy. "They said Cal, that was Mayner's name. Maybe they're following the suits and not us."

"Whatever," he said. "I can't say that I'm more pleased by that possibility, it's still two lots hanging around, either of which, or both of them, might be up to no good."

He was right, there might be only one lot of criminals to worry about. Mind you, if we were looking for stolen property then the police weren't on our side. But they might come in handy.

The man was still talking. "OK we'll leave it; we'll come back to the station. We can pick them up later." So they were police, or at least official. We gave it five minutes, nobody came back to look for us so we walked back out into the street.

We found a shop where we bought a portable viewer so that we could look at whatever was on the memory card without using the hotel's network. It was the last one the shop had.

"No call for these any more," the shopkeeper said as he took our money. "It's all clouds and networks. What did you say you wanted it for?"

"We didn't," said Cy curtly as he paid. "And can I have a receipt please, for my expense account."

We felt almost lonely as we wandered around Main Street, neither group returned, or if they did we didn't spot them.

"Do you fancy doing the real tourist bit?" asked Cy as we passed an advertisement for the settlers' exhibition.

"Not really." It was advertised as an interactive experience of the life of the first colonists. "Don't you think this is enough of one then?"

"It's enough for me," he said. "I don't really fancy another. What can they do, suck all the air out for realism?"

Then we found a shop advertising Rovers for hire. "I guess this was where she got her Rover?" said Cy.

"The detective said it was the only place you could, let's go in and ask." I pushed the door open.

The woman behind the desk had long blonde hair; I remembered the hair on Trevor's suit. Not that I thought it was hers, I wasn't that paranoid and anyway she looked far too young to be interested in him. I had noticed that a lot of people here had long hair; it was weird, on the station short hair or no hair was the norm for men and women. Here on Mars, it seemed like everyone wore it long. Her name badge said she was 'Lesleigh'.

"Hi," I said. "I want to rent a Rover?"

She looked at me with a 'what do you think we lend them to just anyone' sort of expression.

"What do you want one for?" So I wasn't the only one who could ask stupid questions.

"Strangely, we want to go outside," said Cy, helpfully. "We've been told we can't do it in a buggy."

She seemed unsure as to whether we were both fruit-cakes. "OK," she said. "Can I see your licence please?"

"Do I need one?" I got there first.

"You need to have passed a safety and emergency radio procedures exam," she said. "You should have a normal driver's licence as well as your safety certificate. We have to be a lot more careful with who we rent to these days, after what happened recently."

"What about a mining Scooper qualification?" I asked. "Is that enough?"

She looked impressed. "Do you have one of those? That'll be fine."

I showed her the authorisation card that I had from the station. "Wow, that's so cool," she said as she admired it. "The ring miners are legends."

Now that we were all mates I got on with my interrogation.

"Someone I know rented from you; they said I had to see Hensens Ridge."

"Oh right, well we are the only official rental place; what was their name?"

"Maisie Duncan."

Her face fell. "What, the lady who died? Are you the press? I shouldn't talk to you; my boss said I mustn't say anything about it. We've had enough grief as it is, we've had to change all our systems, it's been really bad for business. Turns out she fooled us all, pretending she was sightseeing and then doing that! Cow! Are you the police?"

She looked really worried, so Maisie had been responsible for a shake-up in procedures, she would have loved to know that everyone was running around because of her. But she wasn't a cow. Actually, she was; a bit. I had merely chosen to forgive her.

"No. Maisie was my best friend."

She went red, it didn't go with her hair.

"Oh, poor you, I'm sorry about the cow thing, but unofficially her antics have got us into a lot of bother. She exposed certain… flaws in our vetting, at least according to the police. They said that we should have spotted that she was suicidal and stopped her going out."

"How could you hope to do that?"

"I don't know." She shrugged her shoulders. "She seemed fine that day, she said that she was taking Mr Chok out as usual, it was a regular thing, since she had passed her tests and his wife had died."

Hang on, I thought, her letter had said that he was too ill to go, best not to mention it.

"So if I wanted to go out," I asked her, "would that be a problem?"

She shook her head. "Not with one of these," she said. "Anyone that drives a Scooper is plainly too crazy to be suicidal, when do you want to go?"

I told her that I was getting organised and that I'd be in touch. "Sure," she said, "we've always got spare Rovers these days but let me give you a tip. If you get a chance, go out on a tour first, you can see the conditions before you commit." It sounded like a scam to extract money from tourists; after all it was only driving a car.

"Thanks," said Cy. "That's a good plan. Come on, Andi, lunchtime."

We picked a cheap place for lunch, after all we were paying this time. The food that everyone else was eating looked excellent and we sat in the window, just so we could see if the watchers returned. We had just ordered when Cy kicked me under the table. "Ouch!" I said. "What was that for?"

"Act calm," he muttered. "They're back."

I turned my head, one of the suits was taking up position over the road; he was on a cell phone. As I watched, one of the other group strolled into view.

"Hello," said a voice; we had been so busy watching out of the window that we hadn't seen one of the other customers approach us. I turned away from the street, it was the nurse from the care home, she was out of uniform. Her dark hair was released from her nurse's cap and cascaded down the sides of her face in glossy chestnut waves. She was dainty, with an intense, dark-eyed expression. And out of her uniform, she wasn't half as scary!

"Can I talk to you for a while?" she asked. I moved seats so she could sit beside me. "I'll go and get my tea first," she said, returning with a half-filled mug. She settled herself while I wondered what she would have to say.

"I'm Shevaun," she said, "but everyone calls me Shev. There's something that I didn't want to tell you yesterday." She acted nervously, looking around and fiddling with her tea.

"You mean while Trevor was there?" rumbled Cy. "You don't need to worry, we both hate the man, we're not on his side at all."

"I just want to find out what really happened to Maisie," I added.

Shev smiled. "I thought so; Maisie was a lovely lady, we all wondered how she had ended up with someone like him."

Looking back on it, so did I. He had been a great catch, or so I had thought; now I was just pleased to have escaped. And full of guilt that Maisie hadn't.

"She would come in in tears; he was lying about money, he never had much even though he was full of talk about the big projects he was working on. She thought that he was gambling it away or something." That tied in with the letter.

"I knew him on Earth," Cy told her. "We played cards sometimes but he was hopeless, it was too easy to take his money. I gave up after a while cos I felt so bad about it."

"I never knew that." I was shocked. "Trevor told me he used to clean you out."

Cy laughed. "This trip's been a real eye-opener for you then hasn't it."

Shev looked worried. "I do hope I'm not saying the wrong things, but Maisie said you were a proper friend, she was really cut-up about whatever it was you fell out over."

Should I tell her the reason or not?

Cy saved me the bother. "It was over a man," he said and she nodded.

"It usually is; was it because you could see what Trevor was really like?"

Oh boy! She was so wrong but I wasn't going to correct her. I just smiled.

"Love, or at least lust, can be blind," she said, it sounded like she had been on the receiving end. She was right there. She drank some tea and our lunch appeared.

"It was nice to have seen you," she said. "I don't want to disturb your meal; I'll be off. I'm on a late shift anyway."

"But you haven't told us anything," I said. She looked past us into the street. They were changing the guard, a suit had walked past the window on his way to take over. Now the two were talking on the other side of the street.

"Right. Sorry, I was looking out of the window. Oh yeah; Maisie and Kim were real mates, they just clicked. He had been in the home since his wife died, apparently they used to roam all over the crater in a Rover and he missed the freedom, hated being stuck in that room all day. Maisie learned to drive, she got all certificated and would take him out for the day. They'd get a picnic and visit all his old haunts." She stopped. "It is him," she said.

"Who?"

"That man, he just walked past the window again, he was at the home yesterday, when you were leaving."

"Was there a robbery yesterday afternoon? At the home?" asked Cy.

"I don't know," she replied. "I finished when you left and they arrived. I don't watch the news but there have been thefts from homes. There's a gang problem on Mars, everyone keeps quiet about it but it's quite lawless here. Those people you saw, they've been before, they're undertakers, at least that's what their business cards say. Our boss has a deal with them; they're allowed to tout for business. We think it's a protection racket. The residents get fed up with them though, always asking if they've got funeral plans and wills or how they're going to pay for everything."

"It must be the worst bit of the job, looking after them and knowing that's all they have to look forward to is hard-sell undertakers."

"It is; you know, Andi, I feel like I know you already, from what Maisie said about you, that's what I imagined you'd be saying. And from what Maz has told me, you're a star on the station."

Hang on a minute. "You know Maz?"

"She taught me," she replied, "all through seniors. She's great isn't she? I wouldn't have trained to be a nurse without her encouragement. I was rubbish at school but she saw something in me, we swap letters, call every now and then, keep in touch. She's mentioned you a few times. It's how Maisie knew about what you were up to."

"Maz is one of my favourite people." I told her how she had helped us so much, getting the café back on its feet and stopping me making a complete balls of it all.

"That's her, she's a legend on Mars. I'll bet she has hundreds of us writing to her. And it was so sad. I'm sorry but I really do have to go, good luck."

Wait a moment, what was so sad? I knew that Maz had said she moved to the station when she found herself alone, was there a story there? I wanted to know but Shev had got up and was heading out.

As she left the restaurant, Cy nudged me. "Look," he said. I saw Trevor and one of the three suits; they had swapped over while we were talking to Shev. They were having an argument, there were a lot of waving fingers. We had finished our food and were about to leave but stayed inside the café and after a couple of minutes they walked off. We came out and went the other way. It would be better if Trevor didn't know we had seen him; I wondered what was being said.

We went round the rest of the shops on Main Street, we bought a map of the city and the land outside up as far as Hensens Ridge; maybe it was where Maisie had wanted to go for a different reason than Trevor thought. The bloke who sold us the map tried to talk us into getting a set of map plotting things to go with it. They looked like the instruments of torture I remembered from school, compasses and parallel rulers and such.

I said no thanks, it would be a waste of money, neither of us knew how to use them. We had the map and the notes, surely that would be enough for some investigating. If I went out all I would have to do was follow the cliffs. How hard could that be?

We debated doing a few more tourist things but we were both tired so we returned to the hotel and sat in the lounge. We could save that for another day, if we had one to waste. Today had been a success; to celebrate we ordered a bottle of rather overpriced local wine. It came in an ice bucket and sat on the table between us. It was going down nicely as we reviewed our findings.

We had got a few results and had a better idea of what might be going on. We had the map to investigate and compare with what was in the notebook page but surely Trevor would be back to see us; we had seen him with the suits so he would know about our attempts to lose them. And he had promised to leave us the solicitor's number.

He showed up at six, looking harassed. "What have you been up to today?" he asked as he got himself a drink.

"Oh we just had a look around, I bought a few things for the café, spoke to the Rover people, we haven't found out anything useful. I've only got a couple more ideas for tomorrow so I expect I can book our tickets. We'll be heading back to the station on the next shuttle."

He almost choked on his drink when I said that.

"And, Trevor, we need to know Maisie's solicitor's address. You said you'd let me know, I haven't got all day to sit around waiting."

"It's at the apartment," he said. "Sorry, I had to go in early this morning and forgot, I needed to call Earth, time differences and all that." He waved his arms about in a vague 'all that' sort of gesture.

"Listen," he continued, "there's all her stuff in the apartment, it needs sorting out, why don't you come over tomorrow and go through it for me; I can't face it. Tell you what, I'll drop the spare keys in here on my way to work tomorrow and you can lock up and push them through the letter box when you're done. If I leave you the address you can make your own way there, right?"

I had an idea. "Can I have your cell number?" I asked. "I wanted to call you today and I couldn't."

"Sure." He flipped open his wallet and extracted a business card. "They're all on there, but I'll be in the office all day tomorrow, just like I was all day today. I didn't even get out for lunch." Obviously he hadn't seen us and didn't know we had seen him.

I was expecting him to stay and have dinner with us again and was ready to try and get rid of him by pleading tiredness. We had a memory card and a map to play with. But he didn't want to. I started talking about the catering supplies I had bought and his eyes glazed over. "Well, I've got to be running," he said. "If you're not around in the morning I'll leave the keys at the desk."

Relieved to be shot of him, we ate another fantastic meal and then we went to my room where we could spread out the map. Why didn't we ever go to Cy's room? It was my fridge taking a beating every night; the cleaners would think I had a problem. As I opened the door, I could see that we had had visitors. Never mind the cleaners, someone else had come in and trashed the place.

"What's happened?" I said, in full stupid mode.

"Please tell me you didn't leave Maisie's envelope here." Cy was as shocked as me.

"Of course not," I replied, feeling pleased with myself. "It's in my bag." I rummaged around; where was it? I was just starting to get worried when I found it and held it aloft triumphantly. Cy rolled his eyes.

"That's OK then, do you really need all that kit on a day out?"

"Don't go there, Cy; just be grateful I was paying attention when you suggested the room might be bugged." That was my recommendation; best not mention it was a rather lucky afterthought.

We tidied up the mess. Our visitor had kindly left the contents of the fridge; we could attend to them once we had put all the drawers and cushions back and made the bed up.

Cy got the viewer out of its box and inserted the memory card. It didn't work, no matter how much he rattled it. "We've been ripped off," he said. "The player's duff."

"At least you got a receipt."

"That was only so I could charge Trevor," he muttered.

"Well, we can take it back if you like. What was your plan for Trevor, Cy? Tell him that you had to buy it to look at the message Maisie left that we don't want him to know we have?"

He was silent. We were a really good team, between us we made one slightly below average crime-solver. And we could rip each other to bits verbally without ever wanting to come to blows. If things had only been different we could have been the perfect couple.

I unfolded the map and spread it out on the floor. "Do you want to do this bit?" I asked. He was rummaging in my fridge.

"Nope, I slept through this lesson," he replied, passing me a gin. "Anyway, you're the qualified one."

All that meant was that I knew where the auto-return button was. I didn't bother enlightening him. He was busy with his own bottle.

"Read me the co-ordinates," I said as I sipped my gin and tried to work out how I could translate them onto the map. I saw that the margins had numbers written on them.

Using the hotel's monogrammed biro I marked the map reference points as he read them out and joined them up. Then I pulled a drawer back out from the desk to use as a straight edge, feeling pleased with my improvisation skills. I saw the point where the lines crossed.

"The first point is the Westen airlock," I said. That was the one Maisie had left from, the unmanned one.

"I know," said Cy. "It says so here."

Talk about deflated. "Why didn't you bloody tell me?"

"You asked for the numbers, I figured I'd let you show off for a while."

I emptied my bottle and put it down on the map over the airlock, resisting the urge to use the drawer for another purpose entirely.

"What does it say next?" I asked. "And for goodness' sake, tell me place names if there are any."

"Drive five kilometres east, following the cliffs," he read. I had to work out which way was east, the cliffs went both ways from the airlock so I only had a choice of two. I searched all over the map and found what must be a compass thingy marked in the corner, well it was a circle with N, S, E and W marked on it. I reckoned that was a clue to its function.

I used the scale and the lead from the kettle to measure off the distance and laid it on the map. Who needed those fancy instruments? The cliffs were not in a straight line, they wound in and out but I made a mark at the five kilometres with the pen. The arc cut the cliffs in a place near the edge of the map. I could see that east was in the opposite direction to Hensens Ridge. If we had to go much further we would be off the map. The places all had exotic names like Hecate and Julius and Mercury, a mixture of Greek and Roman gods and historical figures. I remembered Hecate; it was where Maisie had been found. It was much less than five kilometres away from the airlock, she must have been leading them on a wild goose chase. But the area where I made the mark had no name, maybe it was on the next map, which we didn't have.

"Why is it, everywhere you ever want on a map is either on the fold or the edge?" Cy said in exasperation. "Why couldn't it be in the middle?"

That was one of life's mysteries. Mind you, no-one on Earth used paper maps any more, it was all screen based and seamless.

Mars had no GPS so things were done the old-fashioned way.

"Now we need to look for two clefts in the rock. It starts off like a wide canyon, just inside it splits, one wide bit, the other one is more of a thin crack," Cy read from the page.

I looked at the sheet, there were loads of canyons marked but one right on the line, a wide one and a thin one with a single entrance was right up against the margin. "Got it," I said.

"It says that it's in the narrow one, about fifty paces down on the left, there's a rock that looks like a face and underneath it is a hole. The stuff is covered with pebbles."

That had been remarkably easy, even for two people who had no clue what the hell they were up to.

"So all we have to do now is go and get it," Cy said.

"Whilst losing our tail and the police."

"And Trevor! Nothing to it then."

"We've got a bonus," I said. "Trevor's business card; I want to phone his office tomorrow. He's lying about lots of things, I wonder if that's just another."

"Let's keep the map and all the papers on us when we go out," suggested Cy. "I don't trust this room as a secure place. It's been turned over once."

That gave me an idea. "Perhaps we could spread a little misinformation."

"How?" said Cy.

"Write down a few notes, X marks the spot; that sort of stuff, send them off in the wrong direction."

"But they've already looked in here once."

"Go and check your room." He got up. "And bring a few bottles back with you," I shouted as he went out.

Five minutes later he was back. "My rooms untouched," he said, pulling bottles from his pockets. He handed me one; white rum, it would do.

"OK, so what we do is write down a load of old rubbish about the gardens of the care home, paces from the door and under trees, six foot down and all that. Leave it in your room; it'll keep them busy for ages."

Cy laughed. "You're really getting the hang of this," he said admiringly. "Here, give me the pen and paper. I'll do you a treasure map that Long John Silver would have been proud of!"

I passed him the bits and he started, humming contentedly, whilst I wondered who the hell this Silver bloke was.

Chapter 14

To my surprise, Trevor had actually dropped off the keys. I went to the desk when I arrived for breakfast the next morning. The manager handed me an envelope. It was the same as the one that I had been handed by Murph. It had 'Andi' scrawled on it, the same as the other one had and although the writing was different it still brought a lump to my throat. I wondered what had happened to Murph, hopefully he was alright. I went into the restaurant, how come Cy wasn't already here and trying to eat everything?

Then I saw him, he had been running! He had a sweaty tee shirt and shorts on and he looked knackered.

"Where have you been?" I asked him.

"You caught me, I've been for a jog," he puffed, hardly able to speak. "How do you think I can eat all that muck and stay ripped?"

"It doesn't seem to be doing you much good." He looked about ready to expire. "How long has that been going on?"

"Since you moved out and went to live at Derek's, I've been getting up early four times a week and going to the park, five laps and back for a shower before you arrive. I haven't been for a while, with the flight and all the food, I needed to get back into it."

He staggered off for a shower and I got coffee and muesli. I knew he had been exercising on the station, I had thought that it was only because of Greg. Seeing him keeping it up was a real eye-opener. He had changed as much as me, maybe more, only in a different way. Ten minutes later he was back and breathing normally as he piled his tray up.

After we had eaten we took a cab to Trevor's place. It was in a new section of tunnel that had only recently been sealed and developed, at least according to the driver. "All the young executives live down here," he said. "It's a temple to showing off." He started telling us prices and all sorts of details. Whatever else Trevor had done it sounded like he had done alright with this bit of his life.

There were rows of multicoloured boxlike, single-storey structures lining the sides of the tunnel; all with parking spaces outside, some even had gardens with lawns and flowers. Most of the other residents must have been at work as there were few vehicles about and fewer people. Our followers would stick out, both groups of them.

Trevor's place was what my mum would have called dead posh; there was lots of shiny metalwork and bland furniture. The driver had been right, it was filled with all the latest gadgets, stuff we'd only heard about on the station. All Maisie's gear was in a pile, everything jumbled together as though it had already been searched and was waiting for disposal.

That made me very angry, this was more than just a pile of objects, it was all that remained of a life. There should have been more than a heap of clothes and a few random objects dumped in the corner of a room like jumble. What made me even angrier were the feminine articles in the bedroom, the long blonde hairs on the quilt and pillows, which were clearly not Maisie's. Trevor hadn't wasted any time. I thought of Lesleigh, but I had seen so many women with long blonde hair, it could have been any one of them. You would have thought that with me coming over he might have tidied up and got rid of the evidence. Maybe the pressure from the suits was getting to him; good!

Cy wandered off to make coffee whilst I made a start on looking through the pile. I couldn't help it but I folded all the clothes neatly and lined the shoes up in pairs. Trevor could do what he liked with it all after I had gone but I was going to make an effort to respect her things while I was here. It almost felt like she was stood beside me, I could sense her presence very strongly. Best not mention it to Cy, he would be creeped out.

Oh Maisie, love, why did we never try to make up, I said to myself. 'Because we thought we had time,' a voice replied in my head. I knew it wasn't her, just my imagining what she would say but it comforted me because I knew it would have been her response. My mind drifted and I found myself holding one of her tunics close to me, breathing in the faint aroma of her that I remembered so well, willing it to give me an answer. 'What happened to you?' I muttered. This time, there was no reply

In the presence of so much of her, I had forgotten what remained of my anger; it served no purpose any more. I still had Trevor to deal with but I had forgiven Maisie, helped by what I had learned from Shev, the plaque and now her clothes. I just hoped that, wherever she was, she could hear me and understand.

Cy returned with the drinks, he saw what I had done and nodded silently. "I'll leave it to you, if you don't mind," he said. "I'll have a good look around."

I found little of interest in her possessions; there was a box of personal papers in among it all, looking inside there were no bank details or a will. I found no jewellery or keepsakes, photo albums or anything like that. There were just some insurance documents, a few letters and a solicitor's address in Tharsis. That was a shame, if it had been on Earth that would have been a nice excuse for a trip. Then I saw a swipe card for Airlock 3. Wasn't that the one that she had gone from? Clearly she was a regular user. I turned it over, it was still in date. If the airlock was unmanned, the card must be the way to access it.

Then in a flash I remembered the police report. 'Airlock operator contacted' it had said, so was it unmanned or not? Did it matter? Perhaps we should take a look.

I also found a video camera, probably the one she had used to record whatever was on the card. I handed it to Cy. He switched it on. "It works," he said. "That's coming with us." He slipped it into his pocket.

I finished my search. "There're a lot of things missing," I said.

"Will, bank details, jewellery. Anything to do with any money she had. But I found this." I showed him the card.

"So?" he shrugged. "We know she went outside, she had a licence and this was her card to access the airlock. Maybe all the good stuff is at the solicitor's, kept away from Trevor's prying eyes and acquisitive habits." Good point.

"If you remember, Trevor said that Maisie went out through an unmanned airlock but I'm sure that the police report said that the operator had been contacted."

Cy thought about it for a moment. "That's another Trevor lie then, they're really stacking up."

"We have time, let's go to the airlock when we've done here and see for ourselves. What have you been doing?" I asked.

"Taking the place apart for clues," he said, sounding like someone who had found a job he liked doing. "I debated blocking his lav and his kitchen drain; in the end I just jammed a piece of cheese in his air-con inlet, just past the bend, that'll stink for weeks. And I checked the fridge, there's loads of good food, let's have a break and a spot of lunch."

Cy had also discovered a well-stocked bar and we were enjoying a drink from it to go with our lunch when there was a knock at the door.

"Don't answer it," said Cy.

"Why not? We're allowed to be here," I answered. I opened the door and realised why.

The three men who had been following us stood there; looking past them I could see the two I reckoned were police loitering across the street. "What do you want?" I asked.

"Who are you?" one of them asked. "We're looking for Trevor Curtis; do we have the wrong house?"

"He's not here," I told him. "Try his office, Douglas Software."

He looked like he didn't believe me. Maybe he was expecting a blonde to answer.

"Can I leave a message then, my name is Hughes. We've been

doing business and I need to speak to him." He looked past me; saw the neat pile of Maisie's things and Cy, drinking Trevor's beer from the bottle. "What are *you* doing here?"

"I don't think that's any of your business," said Cy, coming to the door. "Like she said, Trevor's not here, try his office."

We got a strange look, they must have known who we were, after all they had been following us, but of course we both had to pretend that we hadn't noticed each other. It was all very complicated.

"I'll tell Trevor you called, Mr Hughes," I said and started to shut the door. I thought for a moment that he was going to force his way in but he changed his mind, maybe he was thinking of the people watching him.

"Thank you," he said.

I shut the door and went to the window. Hughes and another man walked off down the road, past the other watchers and out of sight. One of those then followed them. That left one of each group, watching the door, each other and us.

"That's daft," said Cy, after I had shut the door. "He must have Trevor's cell if he's doing business; he knows that he's not here."

"Let's see where the man is then." Cy called the number on the card. Apparently he was a Senior Software Engineer at Douglas Software. It sounded pretty impressive but might have suffered from a little inflation. He turned on the speaker so I could hear the call.

"Douglas Software," the receptionist trilled.

"Hello," said Cy, in his best executive voice. "Can I speak to Mr Curtis please." There was a pause.

"I'm afraid that Mr Curtis is out of the office all this week. Who's calling?"

"Never mind," said Cy. "I'll get him on his cell, thank you."

He rang off and dialled Trevor's cell, it was answered on the first ring, but only by a message. "Hi, this is Trevor. I'm busy in my office, please call there or leave a message." Cy rang off.

"Proper man of mystery isn't he?"

We finished up our lunch. I had sorted out Maisie's things and Cy carried on with his search of the apartment. He found a small safe against the rear wall but it needed a key to disarm the electronic alarm so he left it alone. Maybe all the good stuff was in there. I could ask Trevor when I saw him.

Before we went, I tried to call the solicitor, but they were engaged. I would have to go in the morning and hope that he could see me.

We had finished up. Cy called a cab. When it arrived I locked the front door, pushed the keys through the letter box and we drove away, carrying our tails with us. I left a message on a piece of paper by the door: 'Mr Hughes wants to talk to you'. I took Maisie's paperwork in a plastic folder.

"Where to?" asked the driver, after I had swiped my payment card.

"Airlock 3 please."

He laughed. "You're not from round here are you?"

"Why?" asked Cy.

"Because you called it Airlock 3," the driver replied. "Everyone local calls it the Maisie Duncan these days, because of that poor girl; of course that's not its real name. It's really the Westen, after the settler."

Would Maisie be pleased to have an airlock named after her? It would amuse her for sure and would be a better memory than a plaque on a wall.

"We heard about that," I said. "What happened?"

"The official line is suicide but I don't buy it," the driver said. "Too many easier ways than that. Why waste money on renting a Rover and getting tagged leaving Tharsis when you have so many other options. You ask me, it was one of the gangs."

We both sat up. "Gangs?" Cy beat me to it.

"Sure," the driver continued. "Gangs are a fact of life here, you must have seen them; they all wear suits. They're easy to upset and people vanish, some get found, some not. We get a lot of suicides here. Thing is, a lot of them aren't."

Bloody hell!

"So what do you have to do to upset the gangs?"

"Have something they want and not let them take it. Here we are." The buggy stopped by a steel door set into the rock of the tunnel. It had red lights over it and a large sign. 'Westen airlock, swipe your card and wait for the green light'. On the door was a large number 3 in red.

By the side of it was a small square doorway. "The office is in there," the driver said. "Do you want me to wait?"

We dismissed him and walked into the office.

Inside it was quiet and highly technical; there was a reception desk and behind it a low console and a lot of instruments. A bank of screens showed pictures of the inside and outside of the airlock and a wide glass panel gave us a view of the airlock itself. It was boring inside, just a white walled continuation of the tunnel. The inner door was shut and the outer door was open. There was a man talking on the radio as we watched. He waved at us to be quiet.

"MineCorp two, you are cleared to enter," he said and we watched as a dusty orange coloured Rover came into the airlock. Lights flashed on the panels and behind it the outer door, this one clear, rolled across to shut the space.

"MineCorp two, we are pressurising," said the man, pushing buttons. I could see a read-out, just like the ones on the station and the numbers rose as air was pumped in. They quickly reached one hundred and the inner door opened.

"MineCorp two, clear to proceed." The Rover trundled out into the tunnel.

The man turned to us. "What can I do for you?" he asked. "I'm Charlie and I'm the duty lock-keeper."

I showed him the swipe card. "What do you know about this, Charlie?"

He inspected it. "Where did you get this?"

"It was my friend's, I found it in her things." He swiped the card and read the screen it produced.

"Oh her." He pulled a face. "She's caused us so much grief. No offence, if she was your friend then I'm sorry but there has been such a spate of arse-covering around here that you wouldn't believe."

I reflected that if she had kept her arse covered in the first place none of this might have happened. Then I realised that meant that I would have been on Mars with Trevor instead!

"I'm just trying to make sense of it all," I said. "I was told that she went out when the airlock was unmanned."

He shook his head. "No such thing; all of the locks are manned twenty-five hours a day." It still sounded weird to hear it.

"Do you remember the day she went out?"

"I wasn't here but I can play you the CCTV recording; I know exactly where it is, everyone must have seen it by now. Hang on."

We sat in a couple of chairs and watched the screen. It was split into nine views and was difficult to follow but we could see the Rover enter the lock.

"Can you zoom in on the windows?" I asked. I wanted to see her face one last time.

Charlie tossed us a remote control. "I have checks to do before the next movement, play with this all you want."

"I'd better have that," said Cy. "You're just as likely to wipe it all out, or blow us up or something.

"Thanks for the vote of confidence," I said, I was annoyed but it was probably true. I passed it over. He fiddled for a while. The picture dissolved; the nine views were replaced by one. The Rover drove into view. Maisie was at the wheel, her face was clear, she had the tip of her tongue sticking out. She did that when she was concentrating. Then there was a flicker at her side, just the suggestion of movement.

"Back up," I said. "Did you see that?"

"I did, hang on." He pressed buttons and the scene replayed, there it was again, a flicker, like something vanishing.

"Is that a shadow?" he said.

"Looks more like someone trying to keep out of the picture to me."

Cy played the video back and forward several times but we couldn't see any better, it was only on one frame.

Charlie came back in; he was wearing a suit, the helmet open. "Did you see anything?" he asked.

"We did, is there any way we can get a print of a single frame?"

He shook his head. "I can't release it, sorry. Since it all happened every request has to go through my boss."

"Never mind, are we OK to see it again?"

"Sure, I'm just going into the lock." He pulled the visor down and left through a doorway at the back of the room. Two minutes later he appeared in the lock and started opening a panel. Red lights flashed on the console.

"Give me that remote." I snatched it from Cy and looked at it, there was a 'menu' button and I pressed it. A screen overlaid the image; halfway down was a 'send to remote device' option.

"Here we go," I said triumphantly as I highlighted the video clip and sent it to my email. As insurance I sent it to Cy's as well. Ten seconds later Cy's phone pinged. Mine didn't.

I looked at mine. I had thirty-seven missed calls. I hadn't heard it ring. Looking at the list they were all from Derek and then I saw that my phone was on silent. Oh no, he would think I was avoiding him, I had to call him tonight. But I had got the email with the video clip. I saved it and put my phone back in my pocket. Better not tell Cy about the silent bit, he would only say that I was a silly cow with a death wish for relationships.

I cancelled the menu command on the screen and just stared at Maisie's face. It was slightly distorted by the glass of the Rover's window; it almost looked like there were two of her, one overlapping the other.

Charlie came back in and we thanked him for letting us see the video. "No sweat," he said.

There was little more to say. We knew now that Trevor was lying about the day Maisie went missing, the question was, why? We left the airlock and started to walk back towards the hotel, we had a lot to think about. After a short while we found a cruising cab and flagged it down, wine was calling.

Chapter 15

Trevor timed his call for when I was taking a shower before dinner. Bloody hell! Dripping suds I picked up the room phone, I'd forgotten it was video and had to run for a towel.

"Hi," he said, he sounded worried; there was no leer or reaction at the sight of my disappearing bum either. He must have been distracted by something. Maybe I was losing my looks?

"Why was this bloke Hughes at my house?" he asked.

"Buggered if I know, Trevor," I answered, trying to alter my voice to hide my giveaway. "He just said it was about business." I didn't add, he's been following us since we got here and we saw you talking yesterday so I suspect you know exactly why.

"Oh yeah," he said. "I've remembered what it's about, I'll call him tomorrow." I decided a little probing was in order.

"Well, what's your business with him? He seemed like some sort of gangster to me."

He laughed. "He's a bit frightening isn't he? But he's OK, it's a sales thing, he runs a big company on Earth and I'm writing him software for his financials."

Knowing what I did, that was a laugh. Shev and Maisie reckoned he was a gangster, the police thought he was worth following and Trevor said he was a businessman. I knew where my money was. "Are you coming over for dinner?" I asked him.

"Sorry, I can't. I have to entertain clients tonight. Did you find what you wanted in Maisie's things? Thanks for tidying them, I couldn't face it."

"I got her solicitor's address. Where's all her jewellery?"

"It's in the safe at the apartment, with the rest of her papers, oh shit, sorry, I forgot to tell you. Come back at the weekend and you can see it all."

That was alright then. "I'll go and see the solicitor tomorrow, I expect he'll have copies of all the important stuff; catch up with you later." I ended the call before he could say anything else, I was relieved that I wouldn't have to see him and make polite conversation tonight, Cy would be as well. The more deeply I found that he was involved the harder it was becoming to act innocent. I don't know how he managed to do it.

No sooner had I got back in the shower than the bloody phone rang again. This time I thought stuff it and just carried on. When I got dried and half-dressed I saw the red light on the phone was flashing, I had been left a message. I pressed play and Derek's face filled the screen. Crap! I wanted to talk to him, more than I had Trevor.

And I'd forgotten to call him when I arrived; we'd spoken when I was on the shuttle but that was ages ago. I'd thought about calling him a couple of times and never had. Cy had reminded me, when we had had our difference of opinion over Derek's ex-wife. Derek was sure to be angry with me. And there were all the missed calls, I'd have to apologise. I pressed play and the message started.

"Hello, Andi," the familiar voice said. "I'm sorry to bother you; I guess you didn't call because you're so upset about your friend. I hope you're OK and getting things sorted out. I miss you so much and can't wait to see you again. Now everyone that's ever meant anything to me is on Mars and I'm stuck here. I know it's a cheek but there's something I'd like you to do while you're there, call me. Love you."

I had been so wrapped up that I hadn't spoken to him, he was so understanding and accepting of my failure that I felt guilty and started sobbing. If there was something he wanted me to do while I was there, there was only one real possibility. Never mind me seeing Helen without telling him, I was sure that he was going to ask me to speak to his daughter, Davina. The one who had pulled a knife on me. The one I had put in prison.

I called him straight back and a minute later we were face to face. I didn't understand how that was possible. Light took over an hour yet we could hold a conversation as if we were in the same room, there must be some clever people around to invent things like this. Jess on the shuttle had said her fella had something to do with it, Quantum something, where were Lou or Terri to explain how it all worked in words of one syllable?

"Hi, you," I said. "I was in the shower."

"Sorry I missed it," he replied with a smile, so was I come to think of it.

"I'm so sorry, I should have called you before," I said. "It's been a bit heavy here."

"Sure, don't worry," he answered. "I'm just glad you're OK. I understand what you're going through and I wanted to tell you that I missed you."

That was sweet and I wished that I had the courage to tell him what was going on. I couldn't risk it though, partly because I didn't have a clue if anyone else was listening and partly because I would have to tell him about Trevor and Maisie and our relationship. I don't know why I didn't want to, I knew all about his wife, more than he did himself, maybe I was worried that he might think I was leaving him for Trevor. And I had left it so long, if I had told him at the start it might have been easier. It was hard enough keeping my knowledge of the book from him.

We chatted for a bit about the farm and I told him about Mars. He had never been, even before his wife had left and was fascinated. "I'd love to see how they do what we're doing," he said, "and to meet up with Martin again. But I wanted to ask you something. If you think it's a cheek fair enough..." he stopped for a moment. "I can't ever come to Mars, will you go and see Davina and give her a message from me?"

"If I can," I said, I could always ask Mayner; he might say no and solve my problem.

"Thanks, love," he said. "I know it's a big thing to ask, just tell her that I love her and I'll always be proud to have been her father. Tell her why I can't come and see her; I want her to understand that it's not about her or what she did."

How could I refuse? "I'll try to get to see her and I won't leave it so long next time, promise."

"Come back as quickly as you can," he said as the connection broke.

After that I had to call Maz. I knew it was expensive but Trevor had said we could do what we wanted and I badly needed to ask her something. How could I do that without giving any potential listeners a clue? She was smart; she'd catch on as long as I wasn't too cryptic, little chance of that!

"Oort Cloud Café," the familiar voice answered the call.

"Hi, Maz. It's Andi, how are you?"

"Hello, dear," she said, sounding really pleased to hear me. "How are you getting along?"

"We're fine here," I said. "It's been hard but I'm coming to terms with it all now. I'd hoped to ask your advice before I left but I don't know where to start now that I'm here. I really just called to make sure the café's OK and to say that I met one of your students, a nurse called Shevaun. She said that you keep in touch; she told me to say hello to you."

She gave me a look, then a flash of understanding. She nodded.

"The café's fine," she said. "It's all going smoothly, you're not to worry and rush back. Everyone is doing their thing. Make sure you sort your friend's affairs out before you think about that. Shevaun's lovely isn't she? Real potential there. It's so nice when they keep in touch." She emphasised the name, she had spotted that I hadn't said Shev, hopefully that meant that she understood what I wanted her to do? And keep in touch, surely that was another hint.

Maz rang off and I played the video of Maisie entering the airlock on my phone, it was a longer clip than I had realised, I had saved the whole of the log for that day. I would have to scroll through it to find the bit I wanted. That was a job for later.

Cy turned up, ready for dinner. Where did he put it all? He had the camera from Trevor's apartment. "I thought we could watch this before we eat," he said. "You're looking happy."

"I've just spoken to Derek." I was happy, our relationship was so unforced. I couldn't wait to see him again. "He wants me to do something for him while I'm here," I began and Cy's face fell. "Not the wife thing I hope," he said.

"No, he wants me to see Davina."

"That's different, what do you think?"

"Well she did pull a knife on me but she didn't use it, what she did was wrong but I can sort of understand."

"You have to be careful, just think. What did you say?"

"I told him I'd see if I could. He was very understanding, he didn't want to pressurise me, he's her father and he wants to know that she's OK. He doesn't care what she's done, she's his little girl."

He was dubious. "I understand, I'm just glad it wasn't the Helen thing. Let's talk about it later, once we get a bit further with this." He picked up the memory card and pushed it into the slot on the camera.

Chapter 16

Maisie's face appeared on the screen. "Hi, Andi," she said, she looked a lot older and wiser than the last time I had seen her in person. Her face wasn't flushed and soaked with water for one thing. And there was no surprised guilty look on it.

"At least I hope it's you," she continued. "If it's Trevor then he's won. And if it is Trevor, I hate you, you bastard! I can't keep apologising to you, Andi, but you have to believe that I'm sorry about the way things turned out. Especially as you wouldn't be watching this unless I was dead. And if I'm dead that means we can never make up. Things have happened since I wrote the letter, I'm putting them on here and I'll make sure Murph gets it. I've told him that Trevor will probably get you to come to Mars and he'll be keeping an eye out for you. There's a bloke called Hughes, I think he's a psychopath, I've seen a few in the home and he fits the bill. He's been in to see Kim and scared him witless. He knows what I know so I expect Trevor does as well. I might have to take a little trip soon but I'm going to make it as hard as I can for them to cash in. I have a trick up my sleeve, Kim said that he set it up ages ago and it might work. If you can, keep them away from the face in the rocks, Andi. You have the notebook page, get on with it. Oh, and check with my solicitor. He has a few memories of the old days that you might like, especially that day in the second year at school, just after the Christmas holidays."

The screen went blank. What day was she on about? Why was everyone so bloody cryptic? And why were they better at it than me?

"Interesting," said Cy. "That means that there's more to this than just going out and picking up the loot."

"We're going to have to rent a Rover and go out, you know that?"

He nodded. "I guess. I'm going to have to come with you aren't I?"

"Sorry, Cy. I might need a hand. Maisie went with Kim so it might be a two-man job."

"And I suppose we'll only get one shot at it?"

I reckoned that he was right; at least he didn't seem too freaked about the prospect. I told him my other news. "I spoke to Maz after Derek."

"Why? I hope you didn't say anything that a listener could have used."

"No, I was cryptic, like everyone else seems to be."

He looked dubious. "I was," I insisted. "I've learnt how from listening to everyone else talking. I said that there were things I wished I'd asked her before we left. I told her how we'd met Shev. She said that they kept in touch."

Maybe it wasn't as cryptic as I had thought; he cottoned on straight away. "So we'll go back to that café tomorrow for lunch then. Maz is probably briefing Shev as we speak."

I felt better to know that there might be a way to get Maz's advice, if I needed it. I valued her worldly-wise attitude and her knowledge of Mars could well come in handy. If I was stuck here much longer maybe we could set up a line of communication.

"So," said Cy, "that's all organised. How about Davina, will you go?"

"I have to try," I answered. "I can't let Derek down and Davina never hurt me, frightened me yes but she was scared of Munro's men and desperate to get away. I'll see Mayner tomorrow, after the solicitor, see if I can arrange it."

"Do you think Trevor will grace us with his odious presence tonight? We're getting near the time when I won't be able to pretend to be nice."

"That was the other bit of news. He phoned me about Hughes;

he admitted to knowing him, said it was a work thing. And he's busy 'entertaining clients' tonight."

"Hooray!" Cy was jubilant.

We dined well, the pressure was off, we had a plan.

Chapter 17

The solicitor's office wasn't hard to find. In fact we had walked past it several times when we were trying to bore our followers. I went alone, Cy was attempting to distract the bad guys and we'd agreed to meet up for lunch at the place where we had met Shev.

Mr Bulstrode was the sort of bloke you could have told was a solicitor without the office and trappings. He oozed calm, thoughtful legality, soberly dressed in a three-piece suit, except that it had short trousers and long socks.

I'd had to wait a while to see him but when he ushered me into his office he was charm itself. He sat behind a huge desk, with a green leather top and an old fashioned brass necked lamp on it.

"Miss Pett," he began as tea was served, "I'm so sorry for your loss. I knew Miss Duncan through my aunt. She looked after her at the home and when she mentioned that she needed a solicitor my name sort of came up."

"Thank you," I said, "and I'm sorry for turning up unannounced. I tried to call yesterday but the line was busy."

"That's quite alright, solicitors are few in number on Mars and I wasn't here yesterday anyway. Before I give you the package that Maisie left with me, I need to ask you to answer a question." That was worrying, hopefully it wouldn't be one on sport, I hate sport.

"What was the name of your head teacher at the convent school?"

Phew, it was an easy one. "Sister Grace," I answered, he smiled.

"It's funny how they burn themselves into your mind," he said. "Mine was Father Jerome."

He picked up a large envelope and passed it over to me. "This was left for you," he said, rising. "You can take it all with you or if you want to leave it here that's fine. We can make copies of anything for you if you want them. I'll be outside; just call me when you're done. Probate isn't granted yet but nobody's contesting, it's only a matter of time." He left the room.

I opened it up. In there were all Maisie's important papers, her identity card; bank details and will were on the top. Along with her licences to drive Rovers, both inside and outside the settlement. There was also the business card of a jeweller's shop in Main Street. I looked through the will; she had amended it recently, the ink was a different colour to the body of the document, the new sheets stapled to the back and covered in signatures. Trevor wasn't mentioned at all; not even in passing. As I read on I knew that he would be furious if he knew what was in it, he would contest it for sure.

I was surprised to see that she had left me all her stuff, the apartment that she had shared with Trevor was in her name and now it belonged to me! The deeds were in there, I wasn't an expert but it looked like I owned the place we had been in yesterday. Karma obviously did exist; Trevor must have put it in her name to avoid tax or something, thinking he was clever. Ha! He would love his new landlord.

That meant that I could evict him, bonus! Just wait till Cy heard. And she had left me the contents of her bank accounts and her jewellery. That was touching, I hadn't expected that.

I knew she didn't have any family; her parents had died when we were teenagers and she had no brothers or sisters to leave it to.

Mind you, I would rather have had her and renewed our friendship. There was something else, right at the bottom of the envelope. Folded up, was a blue cotton bag. I looked at it. Whatever it had contained was gone, there were no markings on it to indicate what it might once have held. I felt it, empty. But it must mean something. I peered inside, it looked empty.

I turned it inside out and there was a faint click as a small object fell onto Mr Bulstrode's green leather topped desk.

It looked like a piece of broken glass, about half as big across as my little fingernail. I poked at it with my finger, it caught the light from the desk-lamp and a rainbow exploded over the wall behind the desk.

Suddenly, I knew what the bag had contained; I knew why Trevor was so desperate and what the three suits were hanging around for. Maisie had known it, she had been going out and ferrying them back to help fund a man's retirement. She had been careful not to give the game away in her messages though, just in case.

I picked up what I was pretty sure was a diamond, wrapped it in a tissue and put it in my purse. I took the jeweller's card; put the letter and the video card from Murph and the map with our markings on it back with the rest of the papers. I sealed the envelope and called Mr Bulstrode. I would leave everything here; it would be a lot safer than at the hotel, or in my bag.

Chapter 18

Cy was hanging around outside, nursing a coffee in a paper cup. I'd told him we'd meet at the café. "What's up? Where are our shadows?" I asked. "You haven't brought them here have you?"

"Don't be daft," he said. "I've lost them, they're outside a coffee shop, not the one we went in yesterday, another one I found. I sneaked out the back. Let's get to the café and see if Shev's there. You can tell me all about it."

We strolled off down the road; I could hardly stop from blurting out my news. We sat in the café; it was crowded so we couldn't get a window seat. There was no sign of Shev; we were earlier than last time though.

"OK, spill," he said as we waited for our tea.

"She left me the lot," I said. "Trevor's apartment, I've seen the deeds, it's in her name, all her cash and jewellery, it's as if she's trying to give me back what Trevor took."

Cy took my hand. "I'm pleased for you," he said. "It's just a shame that you never got reconciled properly. Can we shaft Trevor now? Turn him out on the street."

"Not until the will is probated or whatever it's called, the solicitor reckoned it was a formality though. I've saved the best bit." I told him what I had found, unwrapped the tissue and showed him. "Look, it's a diamond, that's what Kim had."

Cy was dubious. "Are you sure?" he asked. "It looks like a piece of glass to me."

"Well I couldn't really ask the solicitor what he thought, could I? Or perhaps I could ask the police, who do you want me to ask, Cy? Maybe I should check with Hughes? Trust me, I know what a diamond looks like. I'm a lady and I've been waiting for someone to give me one for years."

He raised an eyebrow. "Freudian!"

"You know what I mean." I took the card out of my purse and showed it to him. "We can find out properly later, there was this jeweller's card in with it. I reckon he was selling them for Kim."

Shev walked in, uniform on but minus the hat. She spotted us and sat. "Good," she said, "I've been hoping you'd come in. Maz called me last night, she asked me to help you if I could."

It was a relief to know that I had been right.

"She worked out that you had realised that the phones were bugged," Shev said. "It's not the police, the law won't let them. The gangs do it, they listen all the time for people with money or valuables so they can target them or their houses. You need to keep all your valuables with you and never discuss anything important on the phone. And," she added, "you were right, there was a robbery at the home that day. Some people that nobody recognised, they may have been a rival undertakers, it wasn't the three you saw."

"Thanks for coming back," I said. "What you said doesn't surprise me, nothing does about this place."

"That's the right approach," she said. "What can I do?"

That was kind of her and touching that Shev would help us because her old teacher asked her to. But knowing what Trevor was involved in and what had almost certainly happened to Maisie, I was reluctant to take her up on it.

"Thanks, Shev," I said. "But we've got it covered at the moment."

"It might get interesting," Cy added. "We wouldn't want you to get hurt."

"And you have to live here as well, once we've gone."

"No I don't," she said. "I appreciate the heads up but I can go anywhere. I haven't got any ties here, no family. Don't you have nurses on that station of yours?"

I thought back to the infirmary, Heynrik on his ventilator, the nurses tending to him. And Doctor Liz. "Yes we do," I said, "and

I guess you could always come up and give it a try, I could put in a word for you."

"OK, that's settled. I have a late shift today, then I've got a few days off; what can I do?"

"How about following someone for us?"

She smiled. "Sounds easy enough, who do you want me to follow?"

"Trevor," we both said together.

"Oh him." She pulled a face. "I can do that."

"We want to know where he goes. He says he's in his office but they say he's out."

She nodded. "Seems straightforward enough, I'll wear uniform; people will think I'm on home visits or whatever."

I gave her Trevor's home address and business card; she said she would be in touch.

"And, Shev," I said as she left, "please be careful."

She laughed. "I will, Maz would be angry if I wasn't." She sounded more worried about that than anything that Trevor could do.

We finished lunch and went to find the jeweller's shop. We had a job locating it and had to ask. The first few people didn't know; eventually, more by luck than anything else we found it, hidden away in a back street. With our wandering, it looked like we had lost our tail as we stopped outside and peered in the window, through heavy chain link behind the glass.

Then one of the suits appeared, we both saw him at the same time. We started a conversation, I pointed out various rings and Cy loudly said he would get me one of them. We knocked on the door and a camera peered at us. There was a click and the door opened.

The owner came out; he was old, short and bald, he had a deep red groove around his right eye, it made him look strange. The display cases were all covered in metal grilles and a large alarm button was visible on the wall behind the counter. Cameras followed our every move. It felt oppressive but after what we had learned about the place, understandable.

"How can I help you?" he said.

"We have a stone and we'd like to know if it has any value." I passed it across in its tissue wrapping. He held it and looked at me.

"Where did you get it?"

"I'm a Scooper pilot from the mining station off Saturn," I said. "It was in a rock that I found."

That seemed to satisfy him; he opened the tissue and examined the stone. He laid it on a square of black cloth on his desk and pushed a magnifying lens into his eye. It fitted the red groove exactly; he must have been doing this for a while.

He studied the stone, moved it about with a pair of brass tweezers and shone a bright light on it. He was muttering all the time. Eventually he stood up and rubbed his back.

"Rings of Saturn, you say."

I nodded. "That's right."

"Well, someone cut it up before they put it there." He looked at me. "I recognise the stone from its shape anyway. I should do. I made it, from a much larger one. Has Kim sent you instead of the other lady?"

"Kim's dead," I said gently. "And so is the other lady."

"Oh," he replied. "That's very bad news, I'm so sorry to hear that. Then what…"

"They left us to carry on," Cy said. "Will that be OK?"

He reached under the counter; there was a click. "I've turned all the surveillance off and locked the door," he said. "What's your plan?"

Chapter 19

Walking back to the hotel, we felt pleased with ourselves. We had spent a very productive hour with Kevic, the jeweller. He was onboard and we had a route to get the diamonds changed into proper money. We passed the police station. I stopped. "I'm going in to see Mayner, I can't let Derek down, I have to try and arrange a prison visit."

Cy was still dubious. "I guess so, but do you really think it's wise?"

"Yes I do, Cy, he has a message that he wants me to give Davina," I said. "I can't really say no to that can I? Anyway, I want to forgive her. I'm not stupid enough to mention the book."

"With your poker face you don't need to. Don't make me laugh."

"I won't, Cy. Look, I've kept the knowledge from Derek up to now and I kept it from Davina before… well, before."

What I didn't tell him was that I intended to ask Davina if she had heard on the prison grapevine about anyone called Hughes. He would only try and talk me out of that as well. But I figured that it might help shed a little light on the way things were.

"You wait here," I told him and went inside, facing the same chaos as before. Now that I knew it wasn't rowdy pensioners but organised gangs causing the activity I understood the running around, the feeling of helplessness. Especially if the gangs could tap the phones but the police couldn't.

I had to wait for an hour, hopefully Cy had found something to do, he would have to get on with it. In the end Mayner poked his head out of his office. "Come on in, Ms Pett," he called.

His desk was the same shambles, the cups seemed to have bred and the sandwich was still there, its edges curling as if it was slowly evolving legs.

"What can we do for you?" he asked. I felt like asking if he was following me or the people who were following me but didn't want to put his back up. I needed him onside to get my visit.

"Can I get to see Davina Masters please?"

He gave me a look, a sort of 'what the hell would you want to see her for' one. "I don't know if I can arrange that. My boss might not think that it's appropriate given your relationship but I'll see. Are you sure you want to see her?"

"I want to tell her it's OK, I'm not angry with her. Anyway, I have a message from her father. I spoke to him on the station and he asked me." His expression changed at that. I was no longer the victim. I was now a bringer of news from a concerned parent.

"That's different then. Give me a day and I'll let you know. I'll leave a message at your hotel." He didn't ask which one I was stopping at, so I deduced that one of the groups following me were indeed the police.

I thanked him and went outside to see if I could find Cy. He wasn't around; maybe he had gone back to the hotel. He would turn up when he was hungry.

~~~~

Sure enough, as I walked through the door to the hotel lounge he was sat in an armchair, an ice bucket sat in front of him, there was a bottle of wine and two glasses. He was reading a leaflet about the attractions of Tharsis. This gave me an idea.

"There you are," he said, leaning across and filling the empty glass from the bottle. After a pause, he filled up the other, emptying the bottle. "I thought you were bound to have blabbed or confessed to something. I was expecting to have to go in tomorrow and bail you out."

Very funny! "It was manic in there, Cy; it must be what Shev was on about. Anyway, I asked and he'll let me know. It means that we have a spare day tomorrow, what do you fancy doing?"

"I don't know, just sitting around would be a nice change, but we've had a result, my room's been searched."

That was good news. "Did they take it?"

"All gone," he grinned. "It should give them something to keep them occupied."

"If we're going to be collecting the diamonds I'd like to go on a tour. The girl in the shop was right; I need to see the conditions before I hire a Rover. We may get to see where we're going, it could be useful."

"I guess. I don't really fancy going out there as you know, but I'm willing to give it a shot, you need protecting and I feel responsible."

"Thanks, Cy, is that what you're reading about?"

"No, this one is about all the indoor attractions, there's a stack of different ones. There're leaflets over there." He pointed to a display stand.

The stand contained a whole load of advertisements about the things to do on Mars. There were sights to see in the caves themselves. All sorts of pretty rock formations. An exhibition called *The Construction Story*, whatever that was, and the museum dedicated to the first settlers. Then there were the tours outside. I hunted through the leaflets, there was quite a selection. Enough to keep you occupied for a fortnight. To think that I had thought it would be a boring place to spend a holiday.

The most interesting and relevant one for us was a round tour of the crater that the mountains surrounded. According to the little map it went past the place we were interested in and even out as far as Hensens Ridge. I picked up two copies and sat down next to Cy. The wine tasted good, a reward for another satisfying day. We hadn't seen Trevor either, another reason for a glass. I wondered if I could move into my apartment now that I owned it, perhaps I could ask Bulstrode. That would certainly slow Trevor and Miss Long Blonde Hair down a little bit.

The leaflet said that the tour went on all day, lunch was included. On the little colour diagram of the route I noticed that the point of rock that was our objective was called Janus Point.

That was the name missing from our map. "This one will be perfect for us," I said. "We can scope out the rocks so that when we go out on purpose we will know what to look for."

"How big is the vehicle?" Cy said. "Won't it have small windows?"

I read from the leaflet. "The excursion Rovers have twelve seats," I said. "Extra big windows so you can see all around and up to date safety features. They go in the morning or there's a starlight one, we're going to need to see what time it goes past where we want to be so we don't get spotted while we're recovering the loot."

"Let's get on tomorrow's one if we can then."

I was about to call from the public phone in the lobby, then I remembered what Shev had said and used my cell. I managed to book tickets for the next day's excursion before Cy changed his mind. Then we had another good meal, Trevor never showed up and we didn't miss him.

Chapter 20

Next morning after breakfast we went to the airlock for our tour, we walked a few blocks from the hotel and hailed a cab, all the way we kept an eye out to see if our tail had followed. They didn't appear to have, we watched out of the rear window and nobody came after us.

When we arrived at the airlock we found that the Rover was loading up, the man told us it was fully booked as he allocated us our seats. That was good; our friends shouldn't be able to get a seat even if they had kept up with us. This airlock was much bigger than the one we had visited, the one they were calling the Maisie Duncan.

"Great." Cy rolled his eyes as he got a first sight of our transport for the day. "I'm getting better I guess, it must be all the following you around. I'm OK with spaceships and space stations now; I suppose I should add see-through Martian Rovers to the list."

It wasn't just him who was shocked by the sight of the vehicle, I had to blink; it was like a greenhouse on wheels. I'd had visions of something like the Rovers I'd seen on the street of Tharsis only a bit bigger, or the one Maisie had been in but this was completely different.

The passenger cabin had pairs of seats, widely spaced on each side of a central aisle, so there was a pretty good view wherever you were sat and plenty of room for your legs to stretch out. The walls and the ceiling were all glazed, with only a thin metal frame holding it all together. It looked incredibly flimsy. All the engineering must have been hidden under the seats. It was raised up on eight huge wheels, with an enclosed area at the front and the back.

I glanced at our fellow passengers as we entered the cabin. They were all older than us, it almost looked like a care home day out, but everyone smiled and said 'good morning'.

Once we were all settled in there was one seat left, just across the aisle from us. The guide looked at his watch. "Looks like they missed us," he said. "Well, Mr Hughes, wherever you are, that's just tough. We're off, no refunds for no-shows either."

I looked at Cy, his face looked about as shocked as mine must have done; Mr Hughes, how the hell did he know we would be here? He had to be listening in to my calls somehow. Just like Shev had said. I thought she had just meant the land-lines. I tried to think of what I had said on my cell since we had been here, had I said anything that would give anyone a clue as to what we really knew? It had been on silent, so I hadn't answered any calls. "If they can listen to our cells, Cy, what else can they do?"

"We know they bug the rooms," he answered. "Maybe they can rob solicitors' offices or infiltrate Rover hire companies." That was food for thought.

"There is one good thing," Cy added as the engine started up, "Hughes might have a ticket but it looks like he's missed it."

As the door started to shut a buggy arrived and slid to a halt in a cloud of red dust. "Strike that, he's just made it," our guide announced as Mr Hughes appeared and shoved his way on board.

"Sorry about that," he said to the guide. "My cab had a problem. Thanks for waiting." He walked down and sat opposite me. He had the same suit on; it was showing patches of red dust, almost as if he had been gardening in it. Perhaps he had been digging for diamonds?

"Hello again," he said. "I think we met at Trevor Curtis's house, I'm Jerry Hughes." Talk about brass neck.

"We did," I answered. "Andi Pett." There was a rustle of conversation as I said it, everyone turned around and gawped at me; I felt myself going red.

"I thought I recognised you," Hughes said with a smile. "You're famous, aren't you? I believe you knew a friend of mine on that mining station, Jasper Munro."

"That's right," Cy joined in. "We did, I expect you know that he died."

Hughes looked annoyed. "Ahh the sidekick speaks, your picture doesn't do you justice. So, why take the tour today?"

God he was a chancer, I was just about to blurt it out, then I decided to have some fun. I was safe enough in the crowd and I had proved that I could do cryptic.

"My friend Maisie used to come out here," I said. "She told me I had to come and see for myself. She said it was so beautiful, there were so many pretty things to see."

He never flinched. "And does she still? Come out here?"

"No, actually she's dead; she died out here strangely enough." He wasn't biting though.

"Oh dear, that's so sad. If it's any consolation, at least she was somewhere she loved. Dying seems to be an alarming habit among your acquaintances though, doesn't it?"

"Let's just hope Trevor doesn't succumb then," Cy suggested. Hughes was about to say something when we were interrupted by the guide.

"Ladies and gentlemen, good morning, my name is Bob Helve and I'd like to welcome you to this Thar-side tours luxury excursion vehicle. Please make yourselves comfortable as we prepare for your excursion from the city of Tharsis. We'll be touring the Martian crater called Argyre today. We leave behind the tunnels of the city of Tharsis, which we think were formed by lava flow from the three big volcanoes of the Tharsis bulge, that's Ascraeus Mons, Pavonis Mons and Arsia Mons, many millennia ago. As we seal up and enter the airlock," the doors shut and we moved forward as he spoke, "I'd like you all to read the safety card in the seat pocket in front of you."

And a fat lot of good might it do you, I thought. I looked around for a box of corks under the seat; nothing, perhaps the pilot had them? Maybe we could put the safety card over a hole; the pressure of the oxygen draining out might keep it there for a while.

Bob went on to point out the exits and the stowage for survival suits, neglecting to mention that we wouldn't have time to get them out and put them on in the event of depressurisation. As Mayner had said, we had thirty seconds.

Was I alone in knowing that?

The airlock we drove into was a larger copy of the one Maisie had used, a big digital display showed the atmosphere percentage falling as we prepared to exit. The outer door was transparent, by craning my neck I could see an uninterrupted view across a red plain, dotted with rocks, to a horizon of low cliffs. After the tunnels it felt liberating to be going somewhere without a roof, a bit of sky after the enclosed greyness of virtual cloud.

The view out of the side windows was panoramic as we left the safety of the airlock and trundled slowly onto the surface of the crater. Most of the passengers gasped at the lack of a ceiling over their heads, I noticed that Hughes went quiet and sank down in his seat, as if retreating from the openness of it. The sun was up, a lot smaller than it looked on Earth and the lack of atmosphere meant that it provided little heat. You could look straight at it quite comfortably. Everything was red, but not a boring uniform red, there were just as many shades of red as there were greens on Earth. It was achingly beautiful after the claustrophobic tunnels. Our guide was talking again.

"We'll be travelling eastwards at around thirty kilometres an hour, folks. As you may know Mars has no magnetic field so when we say east we mean that we're travelling towards the direction of the sunrise. On your left is the old airlock used by the first settlers, before the tunnels were extended and widened. We wouldn't fit into it in this vehicle but it's still used for small craft."

That was where Maisie had set out from, where we had seen the video. I kicked Cy.

Bob carried on. "Rather confusingly, it's known as the Westen airlock, even though it's at the eastern side of the settlement, if you see what I mean. It's actually named after Bryony Westen, the first female settler, over time the name seems to have been changed on a lot of official papers to Western."

Hughes was watching a dust devil on the other side of the vehicle, out in the crater. He seemed to have ended up sitting next to a talker, a lady of a certain age who kept distracting him from keeping an eye on us. She had a slightly out of fashion tailored suit, chopped blonde hair and skinny booted legs protruding from some sort of shawl.

"Poor bugger," muttered Cy out of the side of this mouth. "He's got a Judy."

I'd never heard of that before. "A what?" I whispered.

"A Judy," he repeated. "An annoying older woman who thinks she's still got it." I understood straight away, they had been some of my best customers in the old days. The sort that thought they looked thirty when in reality they wouldn't see forty if you gave them a mirror. I had tried to be nice to them even though they were irritating and made it obvious that they were better than me, at least in their heads.

"But why call them Judys?" I was confused.

"Because they make me want to punch them," he said, rather unkindly. It made me grin.

"We just passed the old airlock. Five K," I whispered and he nodded. Ten minutes, I thought. Bloody hell! I'd managed to work it out in my head. It might even be right.

"Five K at this speed is ten minutes," said Cy. "I thought I'd better tell you." It wasn't worth biting, he'd never believe me.

We were headed in a straight line, the cliffs advanced and receded from us and after the ten minutes were up they were a blur in the distance. We were not close enough to see any detail in them. Blast! Then about a minute later they started to get closer, huge mountains towered over us, split with canyons and crevices. They were multicoloured, all that was missing were eagles flying over them and cactus plants, you would have been back in the old West I remembered from Saturday afternoon movies.

The guide kept up a running commentary. "We're just passing Janus Point, folks," he said. "We don't get any closer to the cliffs because of the risk of rock falls, but it's over there in all its glory, the promontory sticks out into the crater for quite a distance. It's so named because it used to mark the transition from the Tharsis settlement to the unexplored region of the crater. And of course, Janus was the Roman God of transition, usually shown with two faces."

Hughes had extracted himself from the attention of his neighbour; he leaned over and touched my arm. "It's so beautiful isn't it?"

"Yes it is," I answered, and without hesitation I could agree with him. I wasn't too happy with the contact though. The lack of air made everything look crisp and sharply focused, every detail was visible now that we had gone past the point we were interested in. And something else had occurred to me, Janus was the God who gave his name to January, you know, that time just after Christmas. Clever Maisie. We were on the right track.

"You could get hopelessly lost out here," he continued, "unless you knew what you were doing." Every word had two meanings and I got the impression that he was playing with me, in a cat and mouse sort of way. It was his way of letting me know that he knew what I was up to.

"As long as you have a map, I expect you'd be alright," I said and he blinked rapidly. Got the message now have you?

"That would be a help, but would it be precise enough?"

Ms Judy shook him by the arm at that point and forced him into a long conversation about something inconsequential. She kept touching him, it was sickening and you could tell he was getting irritated by her leech like attachment. Maybe she had been let out for a day and slipped her carer.

We left the point behind us and headed out into the crater; away in the distance I could see a big orange tent type thing, with a big drill or something off to one side of it. The tent showed up clearly against the red of the cliffs, the letters MINECORP were marked on it in white.

"See that tent, folks?" Bob said. "That's one of the prospecting stations we have scattered over the crater, it's all part of the mining operation. They will be drilling for samples; there's a lot of valuable stuff in the ground here. If we get far enough, we'll pass the OLC station, it's part of the farm set-up that we have in Tharsis, did you know that we grow enough food for us all and even export some produce back to Earth. The scientists reckon there are all sorts of bacteria in the soil, who knows what they might discover."

We suddenly stopped, jerking forward in a cloud of dust as the wheels locked. "Sorry, folks," the guide announced. "There's a major dust storm dropping over the cliffs ahead, we're going to head back the other way for a bit, keep ourselves clear of it."

Sure enough we could see the dust boiling over the cliffs ahead of us and pouring down towards the crater floor.

Hughes went white and shrank into his seat again, he was clearly petrified. I was apprehensive but curious. Cy, who I'd thought would be witless, was looking bored. The other passengers chattered excitedly, one screamed. Judy grabbed Hughes, which made him jump. "I'll look after you," she said, it didn't seem to reassure him.

The bored delivery of the guide gave it away; he wasn't worried so we needn't be.

"It's OK, folks," Bob reassured us. "The lack of atmosphere means that we're quite safe, the wind won't be strong enough to do us harm but the dust gets into the moving parts and can clog them up a bit. And we can't see where we're going; it kinda spoils your excursion."

What was spoiling it was his use of the word folks every time he spoke. Couldn't they have taught him to say something less irritating at tour guide school?

We started moving again, turned around and went back round

Janus Point and hugged the cliff wall. That meant that the interesting bit was on Hughes's side, I tried to look without being too obvious, but then I realised it was fine, it was what everyone had come to see and they were all doing it. His head was turned away as he looked, forcing him closer to his new friend. We passed the airlock we had come from; we were now heading away from the bit we were interested in. It was time for some more games.

I tapped Hughes on the shoulder. "Don't worry," I said, "it's safe enough over this side of the crater." I pointed to the cliffs. "There are some great places to explore there, like the old westerns on TV, the outlaws always lived up a canyon."

"But then they were trapped," he answered. "Once you knew which one they were in they had nowhere to go."

Hmm, he was getting good at this. Perhaps I'd better shut up for a while. There were a couple more of the tents, except these were turquoise. "These outposts are owned by a prospecting company, folks," explained Bob, "and they're looking for valuable metal ores, a bit easier to get than the ones that the ring miners harvest from Saturn."

I could second that, drilling a hole in the ground was a bloody sight easier than twelve hours fighting inertia, nausea and the intransigence of the system.

We trundled on across a featureless plain. A line on the horizon became a range of cliffs which soon dwarfed us. We were headed towards a dip between two of them.

"Well, folks," said Bob, "this is where we will stop and have our lunch; we're just coming up to Hensens Ridge. This is a place where prospecting is not allowed and you'll soon see why. We've decided that it's so spectacular that it needs preserving."

We stopped by a series of rock formations that looked just like a frozen waterfall. The colours in the rock were waves and ripples of every shade from pink to scarlet, in places close together like pages of a book, in others wide sweeps of contrasting hues. If this was where Maisie had pretended to want to come to, perhaps it hadn't been all pretence.

"And here we are at Hensens Ridge, the results of volcanic action and erosion, as you can see the rock formations are spectacular. We're going to stop here for an hour or so, refreshments will be served shortly, then we'll take a very slow ride up one of the wider canyons so you can see the patterns close up. If you can fold the tables in the seat backs down, we'll bring you lunch."

A trolley was wheeled through the cabin and picnic lunches were handed out, together with hot or cold drinks.

It was a good spread, cold chicken and salad, fresh fruit and bread. We all ate in silence, then the lady in front of me leant over her seat back and said hello.

"You're remarkably clever, Andorra," she said. "How you fooled that girl into confessing like that."

I blushed. "It was nothing, just a bit of luck really."

"Nonsense," she said, "you're obviously smart, dear. Tell me, are you on a case here?"

She must have been a teacher, maybe she was Maz's sister. "No!" I blurted out. "My friend died here recently and I've come to pay my respects, here was one of her favourite places."

"Oh, I'm sorry," she sounded like she really was as well. "I hope you don't mind me asking but was that the lady who took her life?"

"Yes it was," I answered, was it common knowledge?

"We all thought it was strange," she said. "Such a caring girl, doing the job she did. You must know her partner, Trevor. He came to our home and talked about funeral plans, just after that had happened as well. It must have been so hard for him to carry on talking about such things, poor man."

Beside me Hughes seemed to have a coughing fit, the Judy was slapping him on the back. Cy had gone into trying not to laugh mode, or was it cry? His eyebrows were heading for the back of his head. We both must have been thinking the same; Trevor had told us he was a software programmer and the business card he had given us said it, Douglas Software. So where did going to care homes and talking about funerals fit in with that? No wonder Hughes was coughing, it exposed a lot of what he had told us as lies.

We finished lunch, the food was cleared away and we set off again, up one of the canyons. This one had room to turn the Rover around comfortably. I had the feeling the one we wanted would be a little more claustrophobic.

"You can see the effects of weathering on the layers of rock, folks," Bob said as we drove under an overhang. "The softer sandstones and the harder volcanic rocks have worn at different rates." Lights came on, pointing at the rock and the shadows cast by our motion looked just like a whole lot of people running away from us. There were gasps from everyone, it was quite eerie. "We call this place the valley of the moving crowd," said Bob as we swung around. We drove back down the canyon in deepening gloom, emerging into the crater in deep shadows as the sun dropped below the cliffs. "Now we just have to get home before it gets too dark."

The sun was setting as we drove into the airlock; it had been an exhilarating ride, chasing the shadows across the crater floor back to the safety of the settlement. As the Rover parked and we all prepared to disembark, Hughes turned to us.

"A very interesting day," he said. "I learnt a lot."

"So did I," Cy replied. "Lots of interesting things." He paused. "Hopefully we've made memories that will stay with us for a while."

He was doing it now.

"It was nice to see you both again," Hughes said. "Maybe we'll meet up again soon."

"We'll look forward to it," I said, his expression suggested that I shouldn't.

When we got back to the hotel, there was a message from Mayner for me. Davina had agreed to see me and it had been cleared by the authorities. I should present myself at the prison gate tomorrow morning at ten. The message said that it was one visitor only. Cy would have to find something else to do. As we crossed the lobby to the lifts I saw Shev, she had her arm in a sling and looked the worse for wear.

Chapter 21

"Hi, Shev," I said. "What happened to you?"

She smiled weakly. "Can I come up to your room and tell you?" She stood with difficulty and limped to the lift.

We rode up in silence. I didn't know what to say and beside me Cy was lost in thought. Had we put her in danger by asking her to help? How could I face Maz again if I had?

We went into my room and she sat on the edge of the bed. "Can I get you a drink?" I asked and she nodded.

"Yes please, a strong one."

Cy had taken up his usual place by my mini-bar and appropriated a bottle, he passed it over. "Hang on," he said, ever the gentleman. "I'll get you a glass."

"Don't bother." She twisted the cap off and drank it straight down in one. "That's better, now before you worry too much I'm OK and this is not what you think."

I breathed a sigh of relief and she must have seen my face. "Anyway, it's not for you to worry, I chose to help and I was careful, pass me another."

I would have to raid Cy's fridge. This was all one-way traffic and the bill would show that I emptied my fridge every night. This time he passed me a bottle as well, he knew not to bother asking me if I wanted a glass.

"There's a lot to tell you so I'll just carry on," Shev said after half of the second bottle had vanished.

"First of all, Douglas Software is in the same building as the undertakers that the home use, the ones that I told you about. It's all part of a company called Douglas Trading, they do all sorts around Tharsis. I hadn't made the connection when I saw the card."

So Trevor could be working for either of them, they might even be the same thing. According to the lady on the tour he was selling funeral plans, that didn't sound like software development. Hughes had choked on his lunch when she said it. And I had my suspicions that Douglas Software or Trading or whatever was only a front for the gang that Trevor owed the money to.

"I was at Trevor's apartment at half eight," she started. "He left at quarter to nine and drove straight to the offices. He went in at nine and I never saw him come out. There's a small park opposite, I stayed there and watched all day. His car never moved, I put a piece of rock behind the rear wheel after he parked it and it was still there just before he left at five. If he'd moved it would have been crushed." Bloody hell; was she a nurse or Shev Bond?

"Did Maz teach you that?"

She grinned. "She might have suggested it in one of her lessons." What subject had she taught? Things had changed in education; I couldn't see Sister Grace teaching us how to follow people, at least not ones that hadn't been dead for hundreds of years.

"Is there a back entrance?" asked Cy.

"Yes, but it leads around the side; there's no parking at the back, he would have to come around to the front so I would have seen him." She was organised. So why was she injured?

"How did you hurt yourself?" asked Cy. That was the question I hadn't wanted to ask.

She laughed. "That was me being stupid, I was so busy watching where he was going that I stepped into the street when he finally left. I was hit by a mobility scooter! Don't worry, I landed on my arse and that's padded. It's only a bruised shoulder and my ankle's a bit sore but a hot bath will sort me out. I got into my buggy and followed him back to his apartment, he didn't stop anywhere. Then I came here to see you."

"You gave us a fright but well done." If Trevor had been in all day and Hughes had been with us then maybe they hadn't fallen for the fake treasure map idea after all.

"I'll carry on then," said Shev, finishing the second bottle. "Gotta go, I'm meeting some friends."

"We'll come down with you," I said. "It's time for dinner."

We said goodbye and Shev left the hotel. As we turned to go to the dining room, we saw that Trevor was sitting in one of the armchairs in the lobby.

"Hello, you two," he said. "Sorry I've left you to your own devices but I've been really busy catching up."

"What have you been doing?"

"I called that man Hughes, the one who came to the apartment. We've been together all day, in his offices sorting out his software systems. Now what shall we have for dinner? What have you been up to without me? Who was that?"

This was going to be an interesting dinner. We hadn't had chance to work out how to try and get anything concrete out of Trevor, we would just have to wing it.

We sat and ordered, I was getting fed up with steak so I had local trout with pesto and salad while Cy went for the seafood plate, a mixture of all the finest that the farm had to offer.

Trevor stuck to pasta.

"The food's amazing," I said. "And I guess, like on the station, it's all home grown."

Trevor wasn't sure. "No, they don't do the fish here," he said. "They can't, no running water."

"They do on the station," I replied. "They have tanks and pumps and all sorts. Derek's going to do lobsters next, he told me about it and I suggested a way that he could get the tanks to behave like the sea."

"Derek told you?" Trevor said dubiously. "And you're helping him design them? I reckon Derek's spinning you a line. You have to ask, what's he after?"

That was a bit rich and I debated whether to ask if that was based on his experience in spinning lines to get what he wanted. And why couldn't I help design things? I wasn't that daft! Cy looked at me and I could tell he was thinking the same but somehow, he kept his thoughts to himself. He was getting better, or perhaps he sensed that this was not the moment.

"I wouldn't know," I said. "I tend to be upfront and Derek seems to act the same way. And people told me that it was a good idea. I don't know, when the bits arrive, we'll see whether it was."

"That's good then." Trevor gave me a look, like he was humouring me. He wouldn't feel so smart if he had known that I could soon make him homeless.

"That company of yours, Douglas Software, is that all it does?" Cy asked. We had a couple of bottles of wine as well and every time Trevor took a sip, Cy topped his glass up. Was he trying to get him drunk?

Trevor looked at him as he plied the bottle. "That's enough for me thanks, I have to drive home. Software's all I do at the moment," he said. "Douglas is a big company, they have a lot of other operations on the planet. They do prospecting and mining and they part-own the refinery. I think they have an interest in some care homes as well. If one bit gets busier they told me that people might get moved around to help out."

He should have been a politician; he had managed to answer without saying much that you could pick up on. Or maybe Hughes had warned him about what we had heard.

"Anyway, I live here. What have you done? You said you were going to do some things while you poked about for information. We need to find the will for one thing."

I didn't want to let on that I had seen the will. Clearly he didn't have a clue what was in it or he would be contesting it and Bulstrode would have known. I wasn't going to tell him; he could stew for a while.

He drank again, only this time, as Cy grabbed the bottle he put his hand over his glass. Cy paused.

"Well I've ordered some new cooking gear for the café," I said. "And I still need to speak to the solicitor but today we went out on an excursion."

"It was full of oldies," Cy added. "And some of them were from Maisie's home, you know the one she worked at. They said some very nice things about her."

Trevor looked pleased. "Everyone I've met since… they all said how great she was. Did you get to Hensens Ridge, or was there somewhere else you went to?" So he was probing as well. "Is it as pretty as she said?"

"It's all spectacular," I answered. "So many interesting places, the shadows make some weird effects. I reckon that the night trip would be just as good, you should definitely go."

"I don't fancy it, outside, it all seems a bit close to the edge if you know what I mean." He drank again and Cy reached for the bottle. Trevor put his hand over his glass but Cy didn't spot it and half a bottle went up his sleeve and over the table.

Trevor jumped up and shouted, "You stupid prat, what did you do that for?" All conversation stopped and everyone stared.

"Oops! Sorry." Cy calmly put the bottle down and looked straight into Trevor's eye. He held his gaze and made a show of flexing his shoulders and stretching his arms out. Then he got up, slowly and deliberately.

Trevor realised that he shouldn't have said that; this time Cy wasn't stopping. He looked at me for support but I looked down and studied my trout. Trevor got up, turned and ran, scattering people and bumping into waiters as Cy ambled after him, not making any effort to get close. I could tell that he was herding him out of the room. The door slammed and Cy returned. Conversation resumed, although there was a lot of gazing and tutting.

"I thought I handled that rather well," he said. "He'll be headed for the lav."

"You were very restrained," I said, putting my hand over his. "I'm proud of you."

"He was getting to me, all that patronising stuff and the dig about Derek, he must think that everyone behaves like him."

Waiters fussed about us, replacing the tablecloth and our wine. "Thank you for not causing a scene," one of them said.

"Unfortunate accident," Cy said. "I'm ever so sorry. Mr Curtis must have lost his sense of humour, I tried to go after him to apologise but he ran off."

He said it with a straight face and it was almost true.

"Now he's gone," said Cy as we waited for dessert, "what do you plan to say to Davina tomorrow?"

"I've been thinking, I must give her Derek's message. Anyway, I want to forgive her for what she did on the station, not the murders obviously but for waving a knife in my face. I was scared."

"Very magnanimous of you," he said.

"And if you remember, she did apologise for Gordie's actions, she tried to stop him and she gave him grief." I had a sudden thought. "I wonder if Gordie is in the same place as her?"

"Whatever, I don't suppose that they'll be getting conjugal visits," he said.

It must be hard for them, knowing they were so close but separated. He would probably get out before her, all he had done was a little burglary.

"Wish me luck, Cy."

"Yeah, of course," he was thoughtful. "Just promise me you won't ask about Helen."

"I don't know much, officially, so I'd be daft to bring it up." It would be far too easy to let something slip; I wasn't planning on saying a word. I was getting good at being as devious as everyone else seemed to be.

Chapter 22

When we could find a cab that would take us, the prison turned out to be a building with a front which was level with the rock-face. It was right at the end of an old, scruffy tunnel. You couldn't tell how far it extended back into the rock itself, or even if it had been dug out. The entrance might have been built over a side-tunnel, or it might have provided work for the first inmates. Whatever, it was surrounded by a large double fence; there would be no rear exit here. It was ringed with floodlights and towers with guards patrolling.

The driver wasn't keen. "I'm not surprised you couldn't get a cruising cab to take you," he said. "You should have got the hotel to sort it, they're used to prison visitors staying and have their own service."

We had been so determined to avoid detection that we had gone into the centre of town before flagging one down. As soon as the first two drivers had heard the destination they had accelerated away. Then all the cabs seemed to have got wind of us and had vanished or driven away as we walked to them.

In the end, one had stopped and been willing to take us. We chatted to the driver on the way, he told us the reasons that no-one would take us. "People often won't pay," he said, "there can be trouble, cabs get vandalised."

He asked us not to mention who we were seeing or why. "It's best I don't know," was all he would say. The place was miles away from the centre of town and I wondered just how far the tunnels extended. It got shabbier and more weed and rubbish strewn as we journeyed on. There were gangs hanging around, looking pretty menacing. "Avoid eye contact," advised our driver.

He dropped us in front of the gates. "I'll wait," he said. "You'll never get another cab to come and pick you up. It'll only be one visitor; I'll keep the other one of you safe, they know me in there."

He pointed across the road to a dingy looking café. "Come in and find us when you're done," he said as we all got out.

Looking at the place I wished that I didn't have to go inside, it had an air of desperation; sort of 'abandon hope, all ye who enter here'. There were two sets of gates for me to get past on my way in. I showed my identity card and was searched at each, pat-down and electronically. After walking across the bare earth I was taken through more locked doors than I had ever seen in one place.

"I'm Henning, follow me," said the officer who was taking me in, it was all he said as we walked down what seemed like miles of deserted green walled corridors. Every few yards, there were side doors, which I guess led to the cells. The things hanging from his belt, gun, cuffs, something that looked like a cattle prod, all swung and jingled as we went up and down more stairs than I cared to remember. On the entire journey I never saw another human. I was ready for a sit down when we reached another door, which was manned; the others just had cameras, now we must be getting somewhere. It opened to his card.

"This is the maximum security wing," Henning said, as we were allowed deeper into the facility. We must be so far back by now and into solid rock, although my sense of direction could have been all wrong, we could have come around in a circle and been one wall back from the front entrance.

"Here we are." We stopped by a small door which opened as the camera over it saw us and blinked on.

I went in and sat on a metal chair, bolted to the floor. I was in a small room with a glass screen in front of me, my face reflected in it. I looked like I'd run a marathon and was sweating, wisps of hair stuck to my face and I pushed them away.

The lights came on the other side of the glass, now I could

see a room like this one. The door opened and Davina shuffled in. She was dressed in a green boiler suit, her wrists and ankles were attached to her belt with chains. She looked pathetic, thin and drawn. She had a black eye and crusted scabs on her face and knuckles. I couldn't tell her father she was like this. Where was the vitality? She had been a bubbly, healthy young woman. She sat, slowly, as if her hips hurt, the chains clanked.

"Hello, Davina," I said. "Are you OK?" It seemed a bit of a stupid thing to say, given her appearance and circumstances but what else was there?

"I couldn't believe it when I was told you were here; what do you want?" She seemed half asleep. "Don't you hate me?"

"I don't hate you, Davina." I tried to sound sincere, I didn't hate her, she had frightened me but I was over it. "I was coming to Mars and your dad asked me to say hello. He had a message for you and I wanted to ask you something myself." At the mention of her father her face brightened for an instant.

"Where is he, is he coming to see me?"

"I'm sorry, he couldn't come but I was here for something else and he asked me to visit you."

"I guess that he wouldn't turn up, because of Mum." I kept silent, we were getting into dangerous territory there; I was only supposed to know so much. Davina didn't notice, she kept talking.

"What does he want that he couldn't write? I expect he wants you to tell me that he hates me too." Her voice was listless and flat. "You know, I'll be fifty when I get out, if I survive that long, it's not a rest home in here. He'll be gone by then and I'll never see him again."

She looked like she had given up, all her spark had gone. She needed to know that someone cared. And Derek did, as only a father can.

"Of course he doesn't hate you," I said, putting all my sincerity into the words. I had seen his face, early in the morning when he woke and just for a second thought that everything was normal. You could see the change when he remembered. "He loves you so much and told me to say that. He tries to understand why you did what you did but finds it hard. He said that there will always be a place for you in his heart. He's not proud of what you've done but he's proud of you."

She looked like she was going to cry, she wiped at her eyes with her sleeve, it came away wet. "Tell him he's the best father I could have had and that I love him, please." She sniffed and I wanted to hug her. I put my hand against the glass and she covered it with hers, the chain stretching tight as she leant forwards. My words seemed to have helped her, she sat more upright

"Five minutes," said a metallic voice above me.

"Thank you for that, I always liked you, you and Terri, you both gave me a chance. It was the others who let me down. What do you want to know?"

"I'm here because my friend died." Her face fell.

"I'm so sorry," she said.

"And it had something to do with a man called Hughes. Have you heard of him?"

She nodded. "I've heard of him. Somehow the top dogs in here, they know what's going on outside. Hughes is a gangster from Earth. He's here representing a powerful criminal family, the word is that one of the Martian syndicates owes his family a favour and is allowing him to operate here. He's on a last chance, he screwed up a deal on Earth and this job is his shot at redemption. He has some of their gang as helpers, there's a search for something and the deal is that the two gangs will split the profits. But I don't know what it is."

Oh this got better. Trevor was in debt to a Martian gang who were doing a favour to the Earth gang. Somehow the Earth gang had traced the diamonds to Kim and then to Maisie.

The door behind me opened. "Visiting's over," said Henning.

Through the glass I could see Davina being led away, she waved at me and shouted, "Watch out for him," as she vanished back into the prison.

Five minutes later, I was on the street, the sliding door in the fence clanged shut behind me. I crossed the road to the café.

As I went in, Cy and the driver were sat at a table, he was in full flow and I realised that he was describing the simulator on the station. Hopefully he had omitted the sound effects, it might put people off their food. The few other customers were listening; over in the corner I spotted Murph. What was he doing here? I went over to him.

"Are you OK, Murph?" I asked, he looked up at me through bruise-blackened eyes. "What did they do to you?"

He smiled at me. "I live around here, I wipe tables every now and then for a meal. Yeah, I got grief from the suits but I told them nuffin. I just said that I gave you a letter from the lady, but they knew that anyway; you really drive a Scooper?"

"Yes I do, Murph," I said proudly. "And tell you what, to thank you for giving me the letter, I'm buying you lunch. Go and ask for whatever you want."

"Thanks," he said and almost ran over to the counter. I went over to Cy. "Hi there, Cy. I'm all done, you want anything?"

"Alright, Andi? The bacon sandwiches here are pretty good," he said. "Get us another tea will you, and one for Wes."

"I'll take you back when you've finished," said the driver. "I hope you did what you wanted… in there."

"I did, thanks for waiting."

"I've enjoyed talking to your partner," he said. "It makes a change to get decent conversation, it's normally all 'where's the nearest toilet?' from the oldies or 'take me to the hairdresser, young man'."

I stood behind Murph as he ordered a burger with everything, ordered myself a sandwich and the tea, then I sat down. I wasn't going to tell Cy much about what Davina had said in front of the driver and he didn't ask. Instead he just carried on his conversation and I added comments as we talked about the station and Scooping.

Murph came over to our table and listened as I described catching rocks and space-walking. His food arrived, from the way he attacked it, I could see that eating wasn't a regular thing. The waitress brought my sandwich over and I realised just how hungry I was. Cy poured me a tea and I sipped it while I ate.

"Do you really do all that stuff?" Murph asked me as I described catching rocks. "I'd love to have a go at that."

"Listen, Murph, if I can do it, you can. All you need is to get to the station when you're a bit older."

His face fell. "All? Lady, I can hardly get across town," he said with emotion.

"How did you meet Maisie?" I asked him. He took a big bite of his burger and chewed.

"She stopped me from getting hurt. I was begging, outside that home she worked in. It was good pickings, with the relatives, they'd give you a few coins. Someone was trying to take what I had. She bought me food, we got talking. I miss her."

So did I. I reached into my bag and gave him a card for the café. "You keep this and call me, we can sort something out." Maybe I could do him a favour one day.

We finished our meal and I paid for our lunch with my bank card. After a lot of goodbyes, we set off and were soon back in the cleaner part of town. "Drop me here," I said as we drove down Main Street.

"You alright?" asked Cy. I nodded. "I just need a little time on my own."

He told me that he would see me back to the hotel. I was going back to see Mayner. I didn't think he needed to know that, yet. I waited until the cab had gone and crossed the road.

Chapter 23

Are you following us?" I asked Mayner straight out. I'd only had to wait a few minutes this time, almost as if he knew I was coming.

"Nope," he said, "but you have come onto our radar. Our POI is a guy called Hughes; he's a known criminal from Earth and he's up here for something. And your Trevor is involved with it. How well do you know him?"

Now there was a question I'd rather not answer. I changed the subject.

"What's a bloody POI?"

He laughed. "Person of Interest, we've been following Hughes, who seems to be following you. Have you any idea why?"

I took a deep breath. "No, Trevor told me he was working with Hughes on some software thing."

He smiled. "Douglas Software is part of Douglas Trading. We believe that it's a front for a gang on Mars. We can't prove anything because there is a lot of legitimate business that Douglas is involved in but we think they have a sideline in scamming people in care homes, among other things."

Shev was right, everyone was right.

"We've seen Hughes and Trevor together a lot but they've looked less than happy recently, there's been a lot of arguing." He tried again. "You didn't say how long you'd known Trevor."

"A while," I said. "Less than I'd known Maisie. Has this Hughes got a record?"

He shook his head. "Hang on a minute, you might be a super sleuth on that space station but here I'm supposed to be asking the questions. No, but that doesn't mean anything, all the best ones have top lawyers and witnesses seldom survive long enough to testify."

Just get him outside in a sandstorm, I thought, or sit him next to a predatory granny; he'll tell you everything.

Mayner continued. "It's weird because the Martian gangs wouldn't normally let people like him live long up here. We think they must have some joint project going on."

If only he knew what Davina had just told me.

He thought for a minute. "And you've just seen a known criminal. Is there anything you want to tell me?" This was getting tricky, even more of a balancing act than the one with Trevor.

There wasn't; I shook my head. I could hardly say that I knew what they're after but I'm going to get it first. On the other hand, it could be useful having them just around the corner, so to speak, especially if I could use them to protect me without them realising that they were doing it. And I was prepared to bet he'd get to hear my conversation in the prison soon enough.

I might need the police when it came to the crunch. Hughes and his merry men were sure to have seen me going to the police station and the prison and by now they were most likely getting upset at the lack of progress. Especially as they were financing our stay, they must have seen the bill from my mini-bar!

It would be an idea to tell Mayner about my planned movements, that way they should be around the corner if we had problems. We would just have to conceal anything we might find until the coast was clear.

"I went out on a tour yesterday," I said and he nodded.

"We know; Hughes was on it."

"That's right, I was thinking that I wanted to go out and see… you know, where it happened."

"That's understandable, did you manage to?"

I took a deep breath. "No, there was a dust storm and we had to turn back, we kept out in the crater away from the cliffs anyway. I was thinking that I might go out in a hired Rover, just me and Cy, to have a bit of a wake. If that's alright?"

He tipped his chair back and looked at me. "Well you're qualified and I can understand the desire but if you do, make sure you follow all the procedures. Let someone know when you go, where you're going, all that sort of stuff. I don't want another load of grief from my boss. Your friend has given us enough extra work. We're monitoring all the movements through the airlocks now, on top of all the other stuff we have to do."

"I will, I know all that safety stuff from Scooping, if I do go I'll do it properly." I stood. "Well I won't take up any more of your time, thank you for arranging the visit."

It was time for a glass or two and a strategy meeting.

Chapter 24

Things were coming to a head now, I had a plan and I hoped that I had organised Mayner to have my back covered. Now I needed to talk to Cy about what Davina had said.

Then all we had to do was work out how to give everyone the slip, go outside, get the diamonds, make sure that the police stopped Hughes and pass the stones unnoticed to Kevic. When you said it like that it was easy, if you said it really fast, there was nothing to it.

When I got back to the hotel Cy was in his usual place, with the bucket in attendance. He poured me a glass without asking.

"I didn't want to bring it up while we were with people; how was Davina?"

"Not good, it looked like she had been beaten up, she was thin and seemed to be deeply depressed. She's convinced that she'll never see her father again."

Cy sipped his wine. "Well she won't will she, don't forget she's a double murderer, she's got thirty years and she killed a man of influence, shall we say. You can bet the word has got round in the prison, she won't have many friends."

That was true, maybe the remains of Munro's operation were after a bit of revenge.

"She did tell me one thing," I said. "Hughes is from a gang on Earth. He's messed up and he's on a last chance. He has to get the diamonds to stay alive. Davina confirmed Maisie's story about the two gangs working together. I went to see Mayner as well."

"You did what?"

"Listen, I found out something; Mayner isn't following us, he's following Hughes, he knows about Hughes and Trevor."

Cy rolled his eyes. "So we have to get the diamonds without Hughes and Trevor seeing us, then we have to get them past the bloody police, you don't do things by halves do you?"

"It's perfect, Cy. The police will protect us from Hughes, all we have to do is get the diamonds."

"Why does that not make me feel any better?" he asked.

"Because you can't see the bright side, we're safe now. Hughes won't risk killing us until he has the diamonds, look how much grief killing Maisie has caused him. Not only that, all the expense of getting us here."

He wasn't convinced. "He'll take them and kill us before the police arrive."

"Where is he going to do that? He won't go outside, you saw how scared he was on the tour. It wasn't just the Judy pawing at him that caused his reaction."

Cy grinned. "It can't have helped though."

"Hughes won't trust the Martian gang to take them from us without him being there, he'll think he's being swindled. They might be working together but they won't trust each other…"

"So we'll be left alone to bring them back inside."

"Exactly, then the police can turn up and save the day."

"Your optimism is touching; I just hope you're right."

So did I. But it was all logical, at least my sort of logic.

"Do you want to hear my news?" he asked.

"Of course I do. What have you found?"

"Well, I've looked at the video clip you sent. The one we got from the airlock. While you were with Mayner."

Oh Gawd! He was going to tell me I was a dozy cow for sending the whole day's recording to this phone.

"Listen, I know I made a balls of that…"

He stopped me with a wave of his hand. "Shh, don't spoil your moment of glory." He picked up the bottle, it was empty. 'Don't keep me in bloody suspenders, Cy,' I thought.

"Let's go to my room," he said. Great, at last I could raid *his* fridge. "We need a bit of privacy." We drained our glasses and headed for the lift.

Cy's room was identical to mine, I beat him to the seat by the fridge and grabbed a bottle. I was going to miss being back on the station with its lack of choice in the alcohol department. There was only potato-peeling moonshine or Derek's homebrew. Cy pulled the camera from his pocket. "I've been carrying this around all day, I wanted to have a look while I was waiting for you but the driver was about."

"I know, was it really dangerous there?"

"It might have been. I think that Wes being around legitimised me, if you know what I mean. On my own it might have been different; there was still an atmosphere."

"I felt it inside the prison, it was so depressing. I guess it should be, as a deterrent but even so. It was good to see Murph again, at least he was OK."

"I thought that I recognised him. Wes said avoid starting conversations. Didn't he say that he wanted to be a Scooper pilot one day?"

"He did, but don't all boys want to be astronauts or cowboys or explorers?"

He nodded. "I guess; he'll want to be a footballer or something else next week. Anyhow, when I saw you had downloaded all the day's airlock movements, at first I thought 'dopy bird', but actually it was good that you did. First thing I did this morning, instead of a run I went to the desk and got a memory card. I put it on the bill. Then I copied the file onto it. It was a lot easier to watch it on Maisie's camera. The fast search is better and once I had a copy I could edit it and mess with it."

He picked up a piece of paper and fiddled with the camera. "I made a note of all the interesting bits."

"Great stuff, Cy."

He smiled. "And that's not all, we have sound as well and that's the crucial bit." He played the video and we watched the screen as the events unfolded.

"This bit's about half an hour before Maisie went out," he explained as a Rover entered the airlock.

"Control, this is Douglas Trading, we have a prospecting job, licence ID Jordan. 429 three POB."

"Control, roger." The rig, a black one, went through the airlock.

Cy sped through the recording; there were a couple of other movements, including a bright purple Rover which shot through as the video raced on at eight times normal speed.

"Now here's Maisie," said Cy. "Listen very carefully."

"Control, this is private Rover." That was Maisie's voice, she stopped for a second and a male voice could be heard in the background. "Tell them it's just you." It was so faint I could hardly hear it.

"No passengers, sightseeing only, licence ID Duncan 375," she continued.

Cy stopped the playback. "That was the shadow we saw, whoever was in there with her. I really had to crank the audio to get that bit."

Mayner can't have heard it or it would have been on his report.

"Now the last bit." Cy played the video again and raced to a later portion, he pressed play.

"Control Douglas Trading, requesting inbound."

"Douglas Trading, hold; we have an emergency situation in progress."

"Control Douglas, roger, anything we can do to help?"

Cy stopped the playback.

"I don't understand."

"Shall I play it again," he said. "I've played it so many times and I'm convinced. The voice on the last bit was the voice with Maisie. The Douglas Rover was waiting for her, they killed her and swapped personnel."

It sank in. "The man in the Rover with her when they went out, he was in the other Rover when it came back."

"Exactly!"

"That means it wasn't suicide. We have to go back and tell Mayner."

He shook his head. "Hang on a minute, only if you've changed your mind about the diamonds."

"Oh yeah!" I'd forgotten about that bit. I'd done plenty of thinking about the diamonds. I knew that Cy was right. Maisie had protected the secret from Trevor and from Hughes. It would be wrong to let either of them get their hands on the stones. Cy was entitled to a share for his efforts, if the thought of the proceeds of crime was too much for me, well I could give the cash to my sister, Tia. It'd help cover the money she'd lost when Trevor had sold the house.

"As far as we're concerned it's all circumstantial," Cy said. "It only makes sense if you know things you aren't supposed to. We'd have to explain, Mayner would probably have us arrested for withholding evidence or concealing the diamonds or something."

My mind was made up. I would do what Maisie wanted, finish what she started. "We'd better get moving then; the fake map won't keep them amused forever."

"If it has at all." Cy was keen now. "The sooner we get this done the better. And the sooner we can go home." He ejected the memory card and put it in his pocket.

"Let's have a good meal and a sleep and do it tomorrow."

We ordered room service; the last thing we wanted was to see Trevor.

Chapter 25

Next morning, we sat down to breakfast in a good mood. I had slept well; the knowledge that we were finally going to sort things out had helped me. We hadn't had any contact with Trevor since he had stormed out, what was he up to?

As we started eating, Hughes sat down between us. He had a plate of food and a cup of coffee; where had he sprung from? Mind you, the restaurant was quite busy. We had been watching for Trevor, we hadn't expected him to turn up.

"Good morning to both of you," he said. "I hope you don't mind my joining you, but as I'm sure you've worked out by now, I'm paying for all this and I thought I'd like to see where my money was going." He attacked his food. We didn't know what to do, should we make a run for it, or just carry on eating?

He looked at us. "Well come on then, eat up, you can't go treasure hunting on an empty stomach and today will be a busy one. And before you consider it, my men are by the door. Come on, eat, before it gets cold."

I glanced at the door, two suits. What could we do? We tucked in.

Hughes watched Cy eat for a second. "I saw the bill and wondered," he remarked, "and there's my answer. You know, all you can eat is not an instruction, it's an invitation."

"There's no need to be rude, I like good food," Cy replied.

"And good drink as well, unless the charming Ms Pett is emptying her fridge every night single handed," he said with a chuckle.

"Get to the point," I suggested, with more bravado than I felt.

"The point... yes, the people I represent are looking for something and we think that you know where it is."

I played dumb. "What are you on about?"

He looked disappointed, like a teacher disillusioned with a pupil who was keeping his knowledge under a layer of self-doubt. "Come now, the famous Andorra Pett and you expect me to believe that you haven't worked it out?"

So it was cards on the table time. Alright, I had a few myself.

"Where's your new employee Trevor been hiding? We haven't seen him for a while."

Hughes smiled, well it was more of an evil grin. "You see what I mean, you have worked it out. Don't worry about Trevor. We've been keeping him busy, he owes associates of mine a lot of money and he's trying to pay it off."

"So is it software or funerals or something else that's keeping him busy?"

Before he could answer, or I could ask him why Maisie had to die, four suited figures walked into the restaurant. They took up position around our table; everyone else in the room noticed but pretended that they weren't looking.

"Good, our transport has arrived; I can explain everything on the way. Finish your breakfasts, then please come with me and don't make a fuss." Hughes stood as he spoke.

"What, so we can end up like Maisie, asleep against a rock?"

He shook his head. "Of course not, that was... unfortunate and was not my doing. Those responsible have been shown the error of their ways. I'm very sorry it happened, if that's any consolation. I know she was a good friend of yours. Now we have to get moving, there are things to do."

I looked at Cy, hoping for a bright idea, he shrugged and got up. "I suppose we'd better do what he says," he suggested. That was a great help although I couldn't see what we could do either, there were just too many of them.

"It's nice to see sensible people," said Hughes as we were marched to the door, surrounded by the suits.

The doorman was missing as we went outside; I had considered appealing to him for help. I looked across the street. Mayner's men were watching us, one of them was speaking into a cell phone. Surely they would come to our aid. But they didn't cross the street, just kept watching. Maybe they thought that we were working together.

A black Rover with tinted windows pulled up and the door slid open. We were ushered towards it. It looked very like the one that we had seen on the airlock video. I was under no illusion about what would happen next.

"Hi, Andi," shouted a voice and I turned around, bumping into the suit behind me. He grabbed my arm. The speaker sounded like Shev and was dressed in a nurse's uniform but they had some sort of mask on, obscuring their face.

Hughes turned as well. "Don't get involved, whoever you are," he said.

"We are involved," said another voice. This one was on the other side of me and I looked back; there was another masked person on the other side of our group. Suddenly there were twenty or more of them and they forced their way between the suits until we were surrounded by this new unknown.

"Let them go," said Hughes, the man holding me let go and they all retreated. Over the road, the police were still on the phone.

The new arrivals lacked the suits, some had nurses' uniforms, others were wearing hi-vis vests and working gear but they all shared the same mask.

"You'll regret this, all of you," said Hughes. "We'll get you later." Clearly he didn't want his men to resort to violence with the police watching.

"I'll take my chances with this lot, thank you," I said as Cy and I were moved along the path and into a collection of buggies. I was shepherded into one and Cy into another. We drove off and one of them swung sideways across the road, blocking the traffic and any chance of pursuit. Brakes squealed as the driver got out and dodged down an alley. The black Rover sounded its horn ineffectually and others joined in. I watched out of the rear of the buggy until we rounded a corner.

Shev pulled the mask off. "I can't believe we just did that," she said, her voice trembling. The driver removed his mask, he was rather a dish actually, he grinned.

"That certainly beats mucking the cows out for OLC," he said. "Hi, Andi. I'm Lorrie Squire, my dad's been looking forward to meeting you."

"Will someone explain what's going on?" I asked, my head was spinning; where had this lot come from, how had they known? I smelt Maz but she was eight hundred million miles away.

"We're the rescue party," Shev said. "Wait till we get you safely hidden on the farm and I'll explain everything."

It felt like we drove through most of the tunnels that made up Tharsis but the black vehicle never reappeared. Eventually we arrived at a side tunnel with a wire netting fence and a gate guarding it. There was a sign, 'OLC Tharsis, no admittance without prior authorisation'. Lorrie blew two blasts on the horn; a man came out of a small hut and opened the gate for us.

We drove into a huge cave; it seemed to stretch forever and was the duplicate of the farming levels on the station. We passed fields of crops and livestock, heading towards a collection of buildings in the far corner of the cave. The air smelt of earth and it was a lot more humid. There was running water and lots of people doing things. They all waved as we passed.

It was a relief to have been rescued, but how had this all happened? We stopped in front of the largest of the buildings. I got out. Cy walked over to me.

"Turned out alright then," he said. "Was I glad to get away from that Hughes creature."

An older man came out of the building and walked towards us. "You must be Andi," he said, taking my hand. "I'm Martin Squire and you're very welcome here." I said hello but all the time I was thinking, what the hell is going on? He shook Cy's hand and welcomed him as well.

We went into the building, down a short hallway and into what must have been their dining room. The space was dominated by a huge table in the middle with about twenty people sat around it. They made space on trestle tables and we sat. There were pots of tea and mugs were poured and passed around.

Martin sat at one end. "I expect you're wondering what has happened to you," he said.

"That's an understatement," I said and there was laughter.

"I'll tell the first bit," said Shev, she was sitting next to Lorrie and I sensed that there was more than friendship there, lucky girl!

Chapter 26

"It all starts with Maz," Shev began, well there was a surprise.

"We talk a lot," she said, "and of course your names came up. After we met at the care home, I told Maz that I had seen the famous Andorra Pett and she said that if I could, I should help you; that you were there because of your friend. I'd listened to Maisie for months and tried to support her so I knew immediately what she meant."

I looked around; there was a lot of nodding and sympathetic faces.

Shev carried on. "We all know Maz, she taught most of us and we love her, she saw things in us and encouraged us when the rest of the system couldn't be bothered. We all owe her, so when she says help someone, we do."

But did they know why we were being kidnapped?

"I've told everyone here about Maisie and Trevor, the self-inflicted problems he had and how she was going crazy trying to sort things out, I hope you didn't mind. It seemed only fair; if they were going to risk the gangs and help you they should at least know why. We assume that she hid something from him for safekeeping and that you were here to get it before he could fritter it away."

True; but it wasn't the whole truth.

"We want you to get it and keep it from Trevor and the other men. I was coming to see you to tell you about what they were doing yesterday when I saw one of them get out of a buggy and meet up with the other suits. I recognised him from the home and thought that it might be a problem. So I rounded up a few people to help rescue you."

"Thanks for saving us," said Cy. "We would be in deep trouble without you. I don't mean to sound negative but what can we do now, aren't we trapped in here?" He sounded bothered; maybe he thought that we had escaped one mob for another. And would we have to tell them about the diamonds?

I broke in. "Thanks, Shev, it wasn't a secret; it can't hurt to tell everyone now. It's true that Maisie left me a note about some possessions that she wanted me to have."

That was a stretch but I didn't want to complicate things. Anyway, we might not be able to find the diamonds. It wouldn't do to get anyone's hopes up. We could sort the details out later.

"And what did you see them doing yesterday, Shev?" Cy asked. To be honest, I hadn't expected her to still be following them.

"I thought that I'd better carry on watching. You hadn't said stop so I followed Trevor from his place to the offices. A whole load of them went in the black Rover to the back of the care home. They were digging up the ground," she said, "pretending to be utilities men. Trevor had swapped his suit for hi-vis and overalls. The man I saw this morning seemed to be in charge, shouting at everyone and making them dig where he said."

I wondered where they had got that idea from.

"Don't worry about being trapped in here," said Lorrie. "They can't get in here, we have a guard at the gate. Anyway, they don't know where you went. The buggies we used were all unmarked. They don't know who we are. We can get you out in an OLC Rover anytime you want."

"More importantly, we aren't after whatever your friend left for you," Martin said. "We don't care about it, or need it. We're just helping you stay safe until you can get it. We can help you, we're all pretty sick of the way that the gangs have taken over Tharsis."

"I have to get back to the care home," said Shev, looking at her watch. "I'm glad to have been able to help."

There was one thing that was bothering me. "Shev," I said, "before you go, how do you talk to Maz without being overheard?"

"That's the clever bit," she said, "it's all to do with the video calls."

Oh yeah, video, they could hold up words on pieces of paper. But then I found out that it wasn't that.

"Maz was a special needs teacher; she taught us all sign language."

"Bloody hell, that's brilliant," shouted Cy.

"We found out that although the gangs could tap the phones, they didn't have the bandwidth to do video and audio. We talk rubbish and in the background we sign the real message."

If that wasn't typical Maz teacher cunning I didn't know what was. It had certainly saved us today.

"Or if it's juicy gossip," said Martin, "the sort that signs haven't been invented for, they come in here and use the secure OLC lines." I couldn't imagine what he meant.

A couple of the others got up and left with Shev, wishing us good luck as they went.

"Right, the rest of you can get back to work," said Martin. The remainder of the people in the room were obviously farmhands, they grumbled about 'slave-driving bosses' but strolled out with fond looks at Martin. He seemed to be as popular as Derek; he had the same easy style of command and the respect that went with it.

"We'll meet up at dinner and discuss what we can do to help," he said. "Would you like the tour before that?"

It seemed rude to refuse.

Chapter 27

"I can't show you around myself," said Martin. "I'll get Lorrie or one of the others to do that, I guess it might be boring but I expect we do some things a bit differently to Derek."

"I'd love to see a bit of greenery," Cy said, to my surprise. "We've been in among the tunnels since we got here, apart from a day out. I for one am sick of seeing red rocks and just a few straggly plants, I'd love to feel like I was back in a garden again."

Martin looked really pleased. "Brilliant, I'll get someone, just hang on a minute. He went to a small door, in the corner. "Deb," he shouted, "can you get Lorrie or whoever is about to bring the buggy round. Our guests would like a tour."

He came back in. "All sorted, if you wait at the front door a buggy will pick you up."

We walked out. "Do you really want to drive around fields?" I asked Cy. His reply surprised me.

"Yes I bloody do. I want to be reminded that there really are green spaces, cos that's where I'm going with Greg as soon as I get back to the station. As daft as you might think it sounds, I want to sit in the park, or stroll along the observation deck with him and get this rock out of my mind." The strength of his reply made me realise just what he had given up to come and help me.

I put my hand on his arm. "Cy, I really appreciate your being here to look after me. I know you've got Greg, same as I've got Derek and we'll get back as soon as we can, promise."

"I know, you silly fool. I said I'd look out for you when we left Earth and I will, but I want a bit of a quiet life now, just as soon as we've given Trevor everything he deserves."

We reached the front door and stepped through. It was like walking out into the English countryside in June, ahead of us were fields of wheat and corn. Off to one side, fruit trees grew in a grassy orchard, sheep grazed under the trees, their wool had a reddish tinge. In the distance we could hear cows mooing, or lowing or whatever it was that they did.

A buggy stopped, a girl was driving. "Hi," she shouted. "I'm Alice, hop in and I'll take you around."

We got in and set off. Alice kept glancing across at me. "You're a legend," she said at last. "Oh and you too, Cy," she added hastily.

"Thanks," he said, "but I'm quite happy for Andi to get the credit, I'm just the poor sod who bails her out and does all the hard work after all." Alice wasn't sure if he was joking or not, neither was I come to that. I was about to say something when he burst out laughing.

"Your faces," he gasped. "We're partners, in it together."

"Usually right in it," I added. "But we don't make a bad team do we?"

Alice stopped by a large barn. "There is one thing that I know Martin would like me to show you, come on."

We went inside and there was a huge clear-sided tank, it must have been twenty metres square, water sloshed about from side to side, it was almost like a wave machine in a swimming pool.

"What's this then?" asked Cy.

"It's based on Andi's idea for a rock lobster pool," Alice said. "She suggested shaking the tank to simulate waves. We thought about it and just put a mechanism in one end of the pool to make waves, it's just a big lump of plastic that goes up and down."

It was so much more logical than my idea of shaking the tank. "And have you got any lobsters?"

"You'll see," she said, pointing. "Look here."

At the other end of the tank to the wave thing were rocks and sand, all red. Lobsters clung to the rocks, their shells glistening. The rocks were covered with them, all different sizes. "How do they all survive so close together?" I asked, was that an intelligent question? If it was, that was two today; I was on a roll!

"Concentrated feeding," Alice replied. "They grow really quickly as long as they have food and they don't have to fight each other for it."

There were racks of other tanks containing fish and what looked like a lot of seaweed; some had running water, some still. It was a much bigger version of the station's farm. Trevor should see this, perhaps he'd believe me then.

"What's with all the weeds?" asked Cy. Alice smiled.

"The weed had such a high concentration of protein, like soya beans; it can be turned into so much nutrition you wouldn't believe it. It's a crop in its own right. We just mess about with it until it looks like something palatable; add a bit of natural flavouring and away you go."

That explained the stuff Cy had been eating but couldn't identify, I wonder if he had realised yet?

We left the barn and got back in the buggy. "Where do you want to go now?"

"Can we just drive into the fields and sit for a while?"

"Of course we can; I expect you'd like a rest, we have plenty of time before food."

Alice parked up between two fields of tall wheat and a grassy bank. Bees buzzed and it felt warm and soporific. We didn't speak, we just walked a little way into the bank; sat under a tree and relaxed.

Chapter 28

Dinner was a noisy meal. Sat on the veranda on huge trestle tables there were bowls of salad and cold meats, cheese, crusty bread and huge jugs of lemonade. And lobster!

"It's all home produced," said Lorrie who had joined us. We were introduced to so many people that my head could never hold the names, but they all had one thing in common, they were all friendly and cheerful, enjoying their life working the soil of this alien environment. It wasn't even imported, like on the station, Alice had explained it to us while we sat on the grassy bank under what turned out to be pear trees.

"We made the soil," she had said, "with all the food and human waste from the city. We composted it and mixed it with local dirt. We're making more all the time, it's what our domes out in the crater are doing. We can inoculate the soil with different strains of bacteria in a sterile environment and see which take."

The food was delicious and soon there was a huge argument going about which farm was the best. Quite a few of the people had worked on more than one, there were five altogether, three in Earth orbit, plus this one and the one on the station. And there were a couple of livestock only facilities as well. The general opinion was that the one you were on was the worst and the last one was the best. I couldn't say, I'd only tried two and they were both better than the produce from Earth.

Eventually the meal was over and everyone started to leave, until we were alone with Martin.

"I didn't get the chance to say it earlier, I'm so pleased to finally meet you," he said coming around the table to sit by me. "You've saved my old friend from torturing himself to death."

What did he mean?

"Shall I go?" asked Cy, aware of my discomfort.

"Please don't leave on my account," Martin said. "Maybe I shouldn't tell you but I thought that you would know. If not, then from what I've heard of you, you'll understand. Derek called me when his wife left him. He asked me to find out where she was on Mars. He wanted to send her a message."

"Oh! I knew about his wife," I said. "And as you probably know I had dealings with his daughter as well."

"Yes, but what you don't know is that I refused to do it for him. He said that it was killing him, not understanding why Helen had gone. I managed to talk him out of searching for her. I said that it would never do him any good trying to understand, she would never tell him why now if she hadn't at the time. He just had to accept that everything happens for a reason. We argued and didn't speak for a while."

I smiled. "And it had turned out that I was the reason."

"That's right. He called me again when you two got together and thanked me. He said that if he had been chasing the past, he never would have found the future." That was sweet; judging from Cy's expression, I might have blushed. So Martin didn't know about the reasons for Helen's leaving, or perhaps he did and just wasn't saying.

"Now then, to business," Martin was brisk. "What about the contents of your hotel rooms? Is there anything incriminating there?"

"No, it's all with us or at the solicitor's. There's just our clothes and toiletries. Any other important stuff is with us."

He sighed. "I'm sorry but we can't go and get them for you, we might be followed, or they might have already gone. We can have a collection from the staff here for essentials, I'll arrange it."

"Thank you, we do need to get out though and not just from the farm. We must finish what we came here for. That means a trip outside, can you help us?"

"That's the easy bit, I think Lorrie mentioned it already, we have an OLC Rover. It's all painted up with our logo. We have some experimental stations out in the crater, so we're visiting them all the time. You'll have to give your ID on the radio when you're in the airlock but by then it will be too late for anyone to follow you. And we can book you a slot, so you don't have to queue. It's just a pity that we haven't got our own airlock but there you are."

I had an idea. "I've had to leave all my notes. They're safe at the solicitor's. Can I get out and have a recce and a practise driving on the crater without anyone knowing that I've been out?"

"Of course you can, in fact we'll be going out tomorrow, what bit do you want to see?"

"Andi," said Cy, "a word."

Martin smiled. "I understand, sorry. It's all happening a bit quickly for you and you don't know much about us. I'll find you a couple of rooms. You can use the phones without fear. They go through the private OLC network and are encrypted. They can't be tapped, unless you have one of our receivers."

That was a relief, I needed to speak to Maz and I couldn't do sign language.

The rooms we got were in the accommodation block and were basic; we sat in mine (again) and discussed tactics. This time there was no fridge for Cy to raid.

"Just be careful," Cy said, "before you go rushing off and showing them where the diamonds are, how do we know that this lot won't take the stuff for themselves?"

"We don't! Cy, I just want to cruise past the area, to spot the double canyon for myself, before we go out for real. It's worth the risk. I can make the driver go past several places and not let on which is the real one. In fact, if he lets me have a drive I can get used to the vehicle as well. And they said that they don't want the stuff."

"But they don't know what it is; they probably think it's just

Maisie's jewellery and a bit of cash. If they knew how much was involved, it might change things."

"I intend to keep it that way; we don't know how much is involved either. Anyhow, diamonds are jewellery."

Cy thought for a moment. "You know what I mean. OK," he said. "It makes sense, I'm sure if Maz is involved they wouldn't dare do anything that might upset her, but greed is a funny thing. If they knew what it was we were going for they might change their minds. I'm going for a sleep, can I trust you not to do anything stupid?"

"Of course you can."

Cy left and I got ready for bed. I should phone Derek, tell him about my visit. Except that I didn't want him to know where I was, in case it got him started on the whole Helen thing. News of Davina would just have to wait.

Instead I called the café. I wanted to thank Maz for her help. Nobody answered, it must be shut. I'd have to try again tomorrow.

Chapter 29

"Are you ready to go outside then?" Lorrie asked me at breakfast. "I'm taking the Rover out to do a crew change at one of our remote stations this morning. It's way out past Janus Point and we'll be gone all day but you're both welcome to tag along. Then we won't be using it for a while, so you can borrow it if Martin says it's OK."

"That'll be great," I answered. "I had to leave all my notes behind and I want to look at a couple of places before I go out on my own. A few minutes driving would be nice as well, just to get the hang of things."

"That's fine by me; if you can fly a Scooper and not get wiped out by some rock then I'm sure you can drive a Rover. You can show me where you'd like to go on the chart when we're on the way."

Cy was staying put. "Thanks but no thanks," he said. "I'm going to call Greg and catch up, then I'm just going to relax away from your permanent drama for a while."

Bless him, he'd miss it really.

I climbed into the Rover; it had an airlock big enough for two people at a squeeze. It felt claustrophobic after the excursion vehicle, the windows were considerably smaller. It was painted bright purple with OLC RESEARCH marked all over it. I would have thought that purple was a bad colour, how would you see it against the red? There were a row of suits hanging up by the lock, I would have to get used to one of them as well; we wouldn't be able to collect the diamonds without them. At least they looked about the same as the ones I had worn when training back on the station. They had air for a couple of hours. If you were careful, that was plenty of time. And Cy would have to wear one, I hoped he knew that.

"It's a bit conspicuous, isn't it?" I asked. "The purple."

"No, everyone sees it every day so nobody notices us. It's only purple so it shows up well outside and that's just in case."

That comment about the colour showed how much I knew. The rest of it was probably true; things that were familiar were invisible. We were ignored as Lorrie drove through the tunnels towards the airlock. We had been joined by Alice, who we had met yesterday, and a bloke called Matt; they were going to relieve two people at one of the outstations. They would be outside, alone together, for three months, which seemed to excite them for some strange reason. The fact that they couldn't keep their hands off each other was a bit of a giveaway. We loaded boxes and boxes of food, bottled water and all the other things they would need to survive out there, along with a load of other stuff that I didn't recognise.

We drove into the Westen airlock, the one that Maisie had used and we had visited. Lorrie explained the procedure to me. "We call traffic when the inner door shuts, give them our ID," he pointed to a plaque on the console, "my licence number and destination and the total on board. Then when the outer door opens we ask for permission to leave. They auto call us every half-hour after that and we just respond with 'situation normal', if it is. It used to be very flexible and we didn't always bother checking in until we got anywhere but after your friend's escapades it tightened up."

"Got it," I said. I didn't let on that I had heard it on tape and read it in the police report. And I was used to doing it when Scooping. When I did this for real I would give my name and Scooper licence number; hopefully that would be enough to alert Mayner, I had hinted enough, he should be listening out for me.

Five minutes later, all the radio traffic was completed, the outer doors were open and we rolled out onto the surface. Matt and Alice hadn't noticed, they were playing tonsil hockey. "Get a room, you two," laughed Lorrie. "Honestly, it'll be nice to see the back of them, they're at it all the time. It's enough to put you off your lunch."

We turned towards Janus Point and stopped. There were a couple of other Rovers about, the excursion vehicle, easily recognised from the expanse of glass and an orange one. I couldn't see the black one that Hughes had been using, which was a relief.

"Right," said Lorrie, he pulled the map out of a drawer and folded it to show the area where we were. It was the same one that we had used in the hotel room. "Do you want to show me the places you want to look at? I'll get us there and then you can have a drive if you like."

"Sure," I said, but I had a sudden panic. Could I trust Lorrie? I hesitated, my finger hovering over the map.

Lorrie took my hand, the contact didn't relax me.

"I understand," he said gently. "You don't know whether to trust me with the location of the stuff."

"That's right, but it's not just you, neither of us know who to trust but then I feel bad because you rescued me, us, yesterday."

"I see what you mean. Tell you what, why don't you drive and I'll answer any questions. Ignore Matt and Alice, they won't be able to remember a thing."

Driving the Rover was just like driving a car, more complicated than a Scooper but without the hassle of dodging rocks. I set off, the atmosphere was clear and I could see Janus Point in the distance. I was aiming to pass closer to it than the excursion had. Then I realised that in the excitement, I had forgotten something.

"Is there a distance counter?" I asked Lorrie, I needed five kilometres from the airlock.

"Sure, it's there," he pointed. I added two to it in my mind; that would be about right, and kept going, angling in towards the cliffs as we got closer. They soon loomed over us and I started to see the physical features. There were hundreds of canyons. I had the drawing from Maisie's envelope in my head and worked back from Janus Point. I had spotted the one I wanted on the map, it was the same as the one we had. Now I had to find it for real.

I drove past several, then spotted one that looked promising. I kept going slowly; that had to be it, a double entrance, it looked the same as most of the others but about twenty-five metres in it split, there was a large and a small canyon inside, just like the notebook page had said. I reckoned that the Rover would fit inside the first bit as well, we would have a lot less distance to walk and be a lot less visible while we were doing it. I tried to etch it in my mind, the entrance shape and the layers in the rock, even the fallen boulders around it. Then I moved up to the next canyon away from the point and did it all again.

"This one's called Hecate," said Lorrie as we approached a tall cliff that stuck out into the crater. "It's the one where…"

So this was the place. I drove in close and looked at the jumble of rocks. I could see the picture of Maisie in my mind but couldn't find the exact one that she had been sitting against.

"I know. I saw the police report. Cy and I want to come back here and have a bit of a wake, say a few words."

He nodded and took my hand again. "Sure, we can supply you with a bottle of wine if you want to toast." That was really sweet and I squeezed his hand, feeling myself well up.

Before I could get too maudlin, I reversed my course and went back towards Janus Point, passing the canyon that I wanted. I stopped at the next for a good look. That ought to be enough to confuse anyone; it was starting to confuse me.

"I saw a picture, I'm trying to get to the place it was drawn from," I explained to Lorrie. "Perhaps it's on the other side of the point." I hoped that sounded convincing enough.

As I rounded the point to start my search on the other side, the radio crackled. "OLC rig, this is Control. Status?"

"Here we go," said Lorrie, "right on time." He picked up the handset. "Control, OLC rig, situation normal."

I drove up and down on this side of the point, stopping a few times for effect. Then I returned to the point.

"OK, I've seen all I want," I said.

Lorrie nodded. "Fine, we'll head for the research dome now then. Shall I take over?"

"Can I get some more practise?"

"Sure, steer 285 on the gyro." That stopped me. How did you do that?

"Two what? Perhaps you'd better take over."

He laughed so much that even the two lovebirds came up for air to see what was happening.

"It's the heading I want you to take." He pointed at a digital readout in front of me, it said 225.

"The numbers increase as you turn to the right," he explained. "Turn the wheel gently and watch." I did and saw the number increase, 230, 242, 250, whoa! It was quick but I got the idea.

"When it gets to 285, straighten up and keep it steady," Lorrie said. He had managed to stop laughing and the other two had gone back to doing what came naturally to them.

After we had that sorted out we passed the MineCorp structure and drove across the featureless plain of the crater floor for about twenty minutes. There was no dust-storm today and the cliffs were crystal clear. A white blob eventually appeared on the horizon, which swiftly grew into a plastic dome, with OLC logos on the walls. It was flanked by banks of solar panels and a small windmill turned sluggishly in the Martian breeze.

"There it is, somewhere quiet for you two," said Lorrie. There was no intelligible answer.

I pulled up outside. "Park in the bay," said Lorrie and I drove into a thing like a carwash, connected to the dome by a covered walkway. My front wheels hit a metal bar and I stopped.

"We're here," announced Lorrie and the one behind us became two; they adjusted their clothing and picked up bags. I saw why we had been stopped by the bars, we were in position for a walkway to extend from the dome and be clamped to the Rover's airlock.

Lorrie called Control and told them we had arrived at OLC

station Foxtrot. Then he changed channels on the radio. "Foxtrot station, good morning, we are in position for the walkway." A male voice acknowledged.

"Do you want to come in and have a look around, Andi; we're only stopping for an hour or so?"

"Sure, why not?"

A couple of minutes later there was the sound of scraping by the airlock, what must have been the walkway landed with a clunk and after another minute someone knocked on the door from the outside. "We have a seal," Lorrie said. "Come on."

We opened the door. There were two men by the entrance, with a pile of crates and cases. Clearly, they were ready to go. There were a lot of handshakes and back slapping.

Inside the dome, it was cool and dry. I don't know what I expected. Maybe a greenhouse type arrangement with harsh lighting; it wasn't like that. There were racks of trays containing plants in various stages of growth, under ordinary strip lights, a curtained living area off to one side.

A large table dominated the centre of the space. It was covered with computers and reams of printout.

"What kept you?" one of the two said, he saw Matt and Alice and nodded. "Of course, I guess you couldn't get them vertical." There was a lot of laughing and the lovebirds looked sheepish. Then they spotted me. "Hello," he said. "Are you a new recruit?"

The other man punched him on the shoulder. "Bryan, don't you know who that is? We're in the presence of royalty!" Hardly how I would describe myself, but I'd take it.

"Bryan, Tomasz," said Lorrie, "this is Andi Pett; she's from the station off Saturn. She's a friend of Derek's and she's here for a look around."

At least they didn't say that I was Derek's new partner. I was fifteen years younger than him and we had got together after his wife left him and come here. But then again, it was always possible that they already knew all that.

"Oh that Andi, I thought you were a bloke," said the one called Bryan. It was so predictable. "You found the body in the freezer and caught that girl, what was her name, the one who killed him."

"Davina Masters," I said, then I wished I hadn't. It went quiet and the temperature dropped.

Alice came to my rescue; she must have removed her mouth from Matt's and started paying attention. "We don't talk about Davina," she said. "Sore point, what with Martin and Derek being friends and the whole Helen thing."

"And we don't talk about the whole Helen thing either," added Matt.

The awkward silence was broken by Lorrie. "Well we can still talk about some things," he said. "Good job really or we'd all be sat around looking at each other. Anything you want to ask about what we're doing here, Andi?"

"What are you doing here?" I mentally thanked him for the prompt. How was that for a sensible question!

"We're trying to make the Martian soil grow things," said Tomasz. "It's very similar to Earth's in basic structure, obviously with the lack of atmosphere there's no worms or life in it." So this was what Alice had been on about.

"But there are anaerobic bacteria," said Alice. "That's my speciality, if you combine them with the amino acids and nutrients that are also present then the dust has everything needed to grow plants, we just need to find some way of unlocking it all."

"Hang on," I said desperately, "can you reduce it to its basics, I'm a dress designer and café owner."

"OK, it's like a scone mix, you put all the stuff together and it won't rise unless you add bi-carb, we need to find the one thing that brings Martian soil to life and lets the plants get at all the good stuff."

Now I understood. "Thank you, why can't everyone explain things in words I can understand?"

We laughed at that and then we unloaded the supplies from the

Rover, stacking them all in a neat kitchen. The living quarters were self-contained in a smaller bulge of the main structure, with a wash room and a separate toilet arrangement. The door was covered with warning stickers; I opened it and peered inside. As well as the seat, there was a mass of equipment, computers and I don't know what else; it was hardly a place for quiet contemplation!

"That's the superloo," said Alice, who had been dragging a single bed from one side of the room to another. "It saves the… product, analyses the bacterial composition and mixes it with Martian soil in sterile conditions, all hands-free thank goodness. The sample is delivered in a container ready for planting."

It was all a bit different to the science lessons I remembered from school, they were just playtime as far as I had been concerned, setting fire to things, making disgusting smells and explosions. I'd managed to set fire to the teacher's tie once, which had made me popular. With everyone but the teacher!

When everything was stowed we sat and drank coffee, I looked at the rows of containers in a new way; some of them were empty while others had tall, strong plants growing.

"What's the point of labelling samples?" I said. "Isn't one… product the same as another?"

"Basically, yes," answered Matt. "Although we all have a slightly different gut flora, the difference is minimal. We're trying to see which plants like the medium best, some do well, others not so. We can tailor our seed selection and grow the best varieties."

To my surprise, I found the whole subject fascinating. Maybe I should have paid more attention at school, there was so much to discover and I had a whole list of questions.

"Sorry to break up the party," said Lorrie, looking at his watch, "but Matt and Alice want to be left alone so they can…" he was stopped by Alice putting her hand over his mouth.

"Enough," she said. "Don't you have to get back before dark?"

With goodbyes we all went to the walkway.

We sealed ourselves in the Rover and disengaged, probably at about the same time as Alice and Matt were doing the opposite! Lorrie backed us out of the frame. "I'll drive back," he said, after reporting to Control.

"That's fine, I'm happy." I had achieved my aims, I knew where we were going and I had driven the vehicle we would be using. And I had learned a few things about the efforts to colonise Mars. All I had to do now was set the date to go out and get the loot. We drove past Janus Point, had one status normal report and then we called the airlock for permission to enter.

"OLC rig, stand-by," the controller said. "We have one outward movement depressurising, then you can enter."

We stopped well clear of the entrance. When the rig was in the lock they called up and I nearly had a heart attack.

"Control, this is Douglas Trading, prospecting trip towards Hensens Ridge, licence ID Jordan 429 three POB." The opposition were about. They couldn't see me, didn't know I was here but their presence made me uncomfortable.

"There's loads of traffic these days," Lorrie explained. "Not just prospecting outfits looking for stuff. As well as the tourist excursions there's the corporate bonding events and the private Rovers. It's why they built the third airlock. Mars might not be as mineral rich as the rings of Saturn but there are a few useful things, iron and bauxite mainly, to be found."

"But they don't go to the ridge," said Bryan from behind us. "It's supposed to be protected as a tourist attraction and a research site, no prospecting is allowed."

The outer doors opened and the vehicle reported and emerged, it swung away to the west, large and black, it was definitely the same as the one that Hughes had tried to get us into yesterday. And I recognised the voice; it was the one from the video.

"Did you recognise that rig?" I asked Lorrie. There was a pause.

"Yes I did, it was the one from yesterday. It's been around a bit recently. I wonder where they're off to?"

I reckoned that they would be following up on what I had told

Hughes during the excursion. If they were searching the canyons, they had a few to go but it meant that we couldn't sit around. Maybe Martin would let us go out on our own tomorrow.

We passed through the airlock and drove to the farm in silence. Cy and I had a lot to talk about.

When we arrived, I helped hook up the fuel and gas lines. I wanted to make sure the Rover was ready for tomorrow if Martin said we could use it. Lorrie had told me that they had nothing planned for it over the next few days, so I was hopeful.

The mechanic, Gus, was standing by to give it a check. "We always have a good look around, plug it into diagnostics, every time it comes back in," he said. "That way we catch anything before it becomes major. It'll be all ready to go out again in the morning."

Chapter 30

"I'm sure that Hughes was heading out to look at Hensens Ridge. I saw the black Rover when we were coming back."

Cy was sitting on the porch of the big house, gazing out at the fields and animals, it was so rural that it was hard to believe we were underground on Mars. It was like a cloudy summer's day in the English countryside used to be.

"Do you know," he said, "I've had a great day. I spent about an hour on the video phone to Greg, had a run around the fields, an excellent lunch, a couple of glasses of wine and a nap. I was almost forgetting the reason why we were here. And then you come back in and spoil it!"

"I'm sorry, Cy, but until we get sorted we've got it all hanging over us. As it happens, I've had a good day. I want to call Derek as well and I've got just as much reason to get back as you have, but if Hughes is searching outside now then we need to get a move on."

He sighed. "I know, but for a minute my life was less complicated. What have you been up to then, did you get to drive the Rover and did you spot where we want to go?"

"I had a drive, it was easy. Well, except for the bloody compass thing but I got that sorted." He looked mystified. "Never mind, anyway, I won't need it, I can see where I want to go. The place I went to was fascinating as well; they're growing all sorts of different plants in Martian soil and they have a really weird toilet."

"And that was the highlight, a weird toilet?"

"It's all connected, Cy, the… well they call it product, is used to activate the nutrients locked in the soil, or something and…" I stopped, having reached the limit of my scientific knowledge.

"Right," said Cy, "I will hold the thought of the weird toilet for a moment while we get back to Hughes. He doesn't know where to look; only what you rambled on about while he was trying to stop that Judy from assaulting him. That made about as much sense as what you just told me."

"He knows it's out there, that's a lot more than he did. Shev said they were digging around the care home. That only kept them busy for a couple of days."

"We have no way of finding out, anyway I want to get back to the station so I agree, we need to get a move on. We can speak to Martin and try to borrow the Rover as soon as."

We saw Martin at dinner. As expected it was delicious. "Is it as good as Derek's?" he asked as we tucked in. Once again, dinner was served from a buffet arrangement; 'take all you want, but eat all you take', we had been told as we lined up.

"Do I have to answer that?" I said. I was getting very diplomatic.

"Of course not, I wouldn't expect you to," he answered, he was very like Derek, calm and charming, in a way it would be sad to leave, now that we had found him.

"Can I talk to you about borrowing the Rover?" I said.

He nodded. "Come to my office after the meal, I'm sure we can work something out."

~~~~

It was late by the time the three of us had finished our discussion and I still wanted to call Derek. I knew I had to, never mind upsetting him, if things didn't go well it might be the last time we spoke. Martin had said we could borrow the Rover in the morning and had booked us a slot in the airlock; all we had to do was bring it back in one piece. Nothing was mentioned about what we were going to get, or where we were going to get it.

Derek was at his desk when he answered the call, I could see the glass doors leading out to his veranda behind him.

"Hello, you," he said. "I've been hoping you'd call, I've been worried."

"I wasn't sure whether to, I'm in the farm, with Martin."

He smiled. "That's great, your being there doesn't upset me. I've spoken to Martin already, he says that you were about to be kidnapped by some gang. What's going on?"

"It's a long story, let's just say it's complicated and I'd rather tell you when I see you, but I'm OK."

"Fair enough, when are you coming back?"

"Soon…"

The picture flickered and dissolved to black, then a little box came up. 'Storm activity' it said, 'signal lost'.

Chapter 31

Next morning I went into breakfast. Cy was already there talking to Lorrie.

"Hi, Andi," he said. "Ready for the off?"

I was just about to say yes when Martin came over. "Sorry," he said. "The airlock called, there's a dust storm outside and all movements are cancelled."

Our faces fell; we were just about psyched up to head out, now this.

"How long do the storms last for?" asked Cy. Martin and Lorrie both shrugged.

"Hard to say, could be a day, or a week."

That was no good at all. "Look on the bright side," said Cy. "If we can't go out, neither can they."

"The phones went off last night, while I was talking to Derek," I said. "A message came up 'storm activity'."

Lorrie nodded. "The dust blocks the microwaves. It's fine and carries a slight static charge, so it sticks to the inside of the dish."

"What are we going to do then?"

"What can we do? We're ready, just wait until we get chance to go out I guess."

The day passed slowly. We watched the local video feed. The storm was still raging and the scientists reckoned it was a bad one, winds of up to sixty miles an hour, which didn't sound as bad as they seemed to think it was.

"Who's the expert on storms?" I asked Lorrie.

"That would be Azelia," he said. "Over in the big barn, behind the tanks; she has a small lab."

"You coming, Cy?"

"Might as well," he said. "It could be interesting."

We walked across through the still air to the barn; it was hard to believe that on the other side of the rock wall there was a storm raging. I wondered about Alice and Matt, had they noticed the earth moving, maybe they thought it was them. We went into the barn, past all the tanks, and found the lab, a small office so full of gear that there was only room for one person inside. Azelia was hunched over a table; all I could see was a mass of dark hair, in worse condition than mine.

"Hi," I said and she looked up, thick glasses made her eyes appear huge.

"Hello, what can I do for you?"

"This storm," I began.

"I know, isn't she glorious? We're due a global but I'm not sure if this is the start of one."

"A global?" Cy said. "That doesn't sound good."

"Oh but it is, they have a three-year cycle. I've never seen one and it's due this year. They start like this, small disturbances all over the planet. Then they join into one big storm that covers a lot of the surface." That sounded bad.

"Until the dust stops the planet warming and they collapse," she added. "Anyway it might not be; winds are dropping a little, only fifty-five miles per hour now."

"That hardly sounds like enough to do any damage."

"It isn't the wind, it's the dust," she repeated what Lorrie had said. "It's statically charged and gums everything up. The wind never gets really strong, there's hardly any atmosphere to move around you see." She swivelled monitors. "Here's the secure satellite feed, it's wired from the other side of the bulge, the storm's not over there. Do you want to see?"

We looked at the planet from space and she zoomed into show us Tharsis, the bulge and the crater took up a large portion of the picture. "That's the settlement," she said, it seemed such an insignificant speck. The dust cloud covered the crater. "It'll move off with the rotation of the planet," she said, "it just takes time."

Time which we might not have.

"Are all movements stopped?" I asked her.

She changed screens. "Look," she said. She had the airlock status page on the government website. In large letters it said that all movements were suspended for the duration of the storm and that no bookings would be honoured until the meteorological office advised that conditions were back to normal. That was a relief.

"Trouble is," said Cy, "if they're waiting for us to go out, then they can carry on searching for us inside."

Chapter 32

Two days later, we climbed into the Rover and I clipped the extra gear I reckoned we might need into the rack. We had been provided with a picnic hamper and a bottle of wine to toast Maisie, after we had done the necessary with the diamonds. There was a hiss as I sealed the outer door. I sat in the driver's seat and started the checks that I had watched Lorrie do.

We had sat around for forty-eight hours while the dust blew around outside. There had been nothing to do so we had tried to chill. Cy ran and exercised. I didn't, I just lazed around and drank tea.

"This is exciting," he said, his tone was nervous, I could tell that he wasn't happy.

"I do hope not," I replied. "I want to have a really boring day, just drive out, get the diamonds and come back in." He had gone quiet and was eying the rack of suits. "Are you alright, Cy?" I asked.

"It's all a bit… close to the edge, if you know what I mean. And you being tidy and methodical, it doesn't scan."

"You'll be fine, Cy, anyway I need the backup. And you came on the tour."

He thought about that for a second.

"OK, you got me there. I was surprised that I quite enjoyed it. But wearing a suit is another step, it bothers me."

"I might need your help, Cy, especially if we have to scrabble around in the rocks for a bag of something. And we still don't know what we're looking for, only that it's diamonds, or part of it is. There might be other stuff as well." I didn't let on that I had worked out what Maisie had meant on the video, about the decoy.

It might mean a second trip and I didn't want to spook him before he had done the first. I could do that later.

"If it's diamonds, they don't take up much space. There won't be as many as there should have been if this Kim was using them to finance his lifestyle." He was trying to be brave, bless him. "Anyway, Maisie got them on her own."

"You're not backing out on me are you?"

"No," he muttered. "I'm just not ecstatic about it, that's all."

I shut and sealed the inner door. I started the Rover up, just like I had seen Lorrie do. Engaging forward gear, I drove across the farm and into the tunnel.

"What do you think we're going to find?" Cy asked me as we slowed for the gate.

"Who knows, a cloth bag like the one in Bulstrode's office? Maybe several if we're really lucky."

The gate swung open and I pulled out into a deserted tunnel, I made my way towards the town and into a bit more traffic. We drove along for a few minutes.

"Do you know where you're going?" Cy asked. "I'm sure we passed this way once already."

"Of course I do," I shouted, did he think I was that dippy? "You just turn down here," I swung the wheel. "Oops." It was a one-way street and I was going the wrong way. So much for inconspicuous. I reversed back onto the main road. "Must be the next one," I said hopefully.

"Do you want to stop and ask someone?" he suggested.

"No I bloody don't; it's around here somewhere."

"Didn't you pay attention last time?"

"Course I did." Actually, I had been put off by the noises coming from the seat behind me and the gorgeous downy hair on Lorrie's arms. But I wasn't going to admit that. Clearly, I had been away from Derek for too long.

"We'll find it."

After about thirty minutes we drove up to the Westen airlock.

I hadn't noticed before but there was a service area just before, a convenient parking place for traffic when the lock was busy. It was in a separate tunnel, hidden from the main road, with slip roads at each end. The light on the airlock was green and the inner door was open so I drove into the lock and saw in the mirror that the door was closing behind me.

"Control, OLC rig, licence Pett, Sierra 67, sightseeing tour, two POB," I said, there was a pause.

"OLC rig, Control, wow, not often we get a Sierra. You sure you're not lost?"

"Negative, Control, just on holiday."

"Well you have a great day, no need to bring us any rocks back," Control answered. Hopefully Mayner would be notified, I had dropped enough hints. And any rocks I happened to get were for me and Cy. I glanced automatically at the pressure gauge on the wall, the numbers were falling.

"When we get back, we'll split up," said Cy. "You drop me in the service area and I'll get a cab to Kevic with the diamonds. Then I can get another one back to the farm. I'm less noticeable than you."

That was true; especially in the OLC boiler suits we had been lent. It seemed like a good plan.

The outer door opened and I asked Control for permission. "Proceed," they said; we set off. I swung clear of the lock and turned towards Janus Point, heading straight for the canyon, which was just to the left of the point itself. I had seen it so many times now that I was quite happy to be out here. Beside me, Cy seemed relaxed. "You OK?" I asked him.

"Sure," he replied. "I'm seeing a different side of you, when you took me out in the Scooper I was too busy trying not to be sick to appreciate your skills, Andi, but you impress me with your professional approach." He said it sincerely, I looked and there was no sardonic grin. That meant a lot from him, he was quick enough to tell me when I fell on my arse, it was nice to think that he could compliment me as well.

"Thanks, Cy, I take this seriously because it is, I can't afford to mess up out here, thirty seconds remember. Here it comes."

We were closing on the cliffs that made up the approach to Janus Point, I altered course as I made out my objective. "There's a lot more dust around," I remarked. "Must be from the storm."

"Has it messed up your view?" Cy asked.

"No, it's just made it look a bit different. There have been a few rocks that have fallen down but we can still get in close." The features were different to what I remembered; they looked softer, even though they were still recognisable.

"Hey, it's just like the drawing," exclaimed Cy as the sheer red cliffs towered over us. I was aiming for the gap I had seen before and soon I drove into the entrance between the two pillars. At least it hadn't been blocked by falling rocks. Ahead was the split, this was definitely the place. I pulled the Rover into the lee of the entrance, now we were hidden from casual view. I switched off the engine and looked at the crevice. It was too narrow for the Rover to get down, we were going to have to get out and explore on foot.

"Now we wait," I said.

"Why?" asked Cy.

"Cos they check up every half hour and we have to answer; as soon as they call we have thirty minutes to get out and back before they call again."

"That's not long; I'd better get a suit on ready then," he said.

We both suited up, Cy put his on like he had been doing it forever. "Where did you learn that?" I asked him.

"I got the girls to show me," he said proudly. "While you were off gallivanting, I thought it would be a good idea." He grinned. "I never would have thought, me in a spacesuit. When you went out with Tina, I took the piss but it was all a show, I wished I had been that brave."

He swallowed; he was sweating as he pulled the helmet on and rotated the lock.

"The idea of nothing; it frightens me," he said. "The idea that I try and breathe in, which is natural, and nothing happens. It scares me witless. I'm still not really happy about going out there; the idea of using a suit worries me."

"And me," I tried to reassure him. "Listen, it concentrates my mind, I know I'm a bit dopy but when it comes to working in space, it all clicks and I think very carefully about everything that I do. Somehow my brain accepts that there's no such thing as a second chance, a laugh and it'll all be alright. I'll check your suit and it'll be OK because this is one thing that I'm good at."

He hugged me, clumsily in the suits. "I trust you, you silly cow," he said.

"Right then, let's get on." I checked his helmet seal. "Now all you have to do is slide the visor down, it turns the air on automatically when it locks."

He nodded. "Got it."

"OLC rig, Control, status?" the radio burst into life.

I picked up the mic. "OLC rig, systems normal."

Chapter 33

"Right, Cy, we have thirty minutes. Come on. It's down the narrow crevice."

I went to the airlock, picking up my equipment from the rack on the way. Cy raised his eyebrows but said nothing.

We locked our visors and went through the airlock. Jumping down, we stood on the red baked surface and looked at the crack in the cliffs. We both had torches and turned them on; they lit up the rocks, forming shadows like the ones we had seen from the excursion. They changed shape as our beams danced together.

We moved deeper into the darkness. "According to the notebook the first stash is about fifty paces in, there's an outcrop shaped like a face, underneath it there's a hole. It's in there."

"What do you mean, the first stash?" asked Cy. I didn't answer. "Come on, we only have twenty-five minutes."

We moved down the crevice in single file, I was in the lead. I counted my paces and kept my eyes open. We had to squeeze past a few outcrops and the thing I was holding made it a bit awkward. I was trying to avoid catching the fabric of the suit on any sharp bits.

"Forty-eight, forty-nine, fifty," I said and stopped. I swung the torch around in all directions but there was nothing. I turned and Cy was doing the same.

"Where is it?"

"I don't know, the notebook said fifty paces."

"Maybe he had longer legs than you? I only got forty-five."

Thanks, Cy, there was no need to remind me that I was short. I moved on, swinging the torch.

When it came it was obvious, a rock shaped like a face grinning out at me from the cliff. It was a natural feature; it only looked like a face when you shone a light on it. The beam threw shadows that made it look so realistic. I walked past it and turned. "This is it," I said to Cy. He bent and peered underneath it, shining his torch into the space below.

"There are two bags in here," he said as he reached in to pull them out. They were ordinary looking leather satchels, brown and unadorned. The leather had dried and gone crusty in the Martian atmosphere as all the moisture had evaporated.

"That's the first stash; the decoy," I explained. "That's what Maisie was going to show them, what she meant when she said about January."

"How do you mean?" Cy had clearly missed out on all the clues.

"Janus Point, Cy. January, the God, two faces."

Realisation dawned. "Ah, then there's another cache under another face."

We carried on down the canyon, Cy in front. I swung the torch and after another fifty paces we saw it.

"There's another face," Cy said. This one was cruder; and obviously man-made. You could still see the chisel marks. The light had less effect.

"Exactly and we're leaving this one where it is." I moved past him and shone the torch under the outcrop. There was another leather bag half exposed and I didn't need to pick it up to see that this one was bulging. I covered it with some more pebbles and earth from the floor, then I used the broom I had brought from the Rover to sweep out our footprints, masking the evidence of what we had been doing.

"So that's why you dragged that along. I thought you'd gone even more fruit cake than usual when you picked it up but then I realised that you must have a reason."

"I'd worked out what Maisie was on about," I explained. "The diamonds were in two places. I wanted to check that I was right without giving the game away, I remembered from old westerns, the outlaws would cover their tracks in the canyons by sweeping them with branches."

He nodded. "So that's where you got the inspiration, when you were winding Hughes up it wasn't all rubbish talk."

Clever old me!

"Let's get back into the Rover so we can have a look at what we've got, we only have five minutes."

"You go first," said Cy. "I'll finish up here." I squeezed past him and moved back down the crevice as quickly as I could. I left it to Cy to rub out our footprints as he went. As I crossed to the Rover I looked at my watch, thirty minutes were up. I pressurised the airlock and as the door opened I heard the call.

OLC rig, Control, status?" I almost fell across the cab in my haste to get the radio.

"OLC rig, systems normal."

"That was a second call," the controller said. "Don't leave it next time, Ms Scooper pilot."

"Roger, Control, sorry about that."

Two minutes later, the airlock hissed as Cy came through it, he carried the broom.

When we had both taken our helmets off, we opened the satchels, one each.

Mine was empty, just dust and a few scraps of cloth.

Cy had more luck with his, there were two cotton bags, the first held a sheaf of banknotes, all out of date now and worthless. "Will you look at that," he said. The faded legend on the other cloth bag was barely readable, 'Swissbank'.

We stopped and looked at each other; this was what we had heard about on the news.

The bag felt lumpy, as if it was filled with pebbles. Cy opened the top. They weren't pebbles, they were bloody diamonds. They were the Swissbank diamonds and they were what all the fuss was about. We danced around, a bit clumsily in the suits but we didn't care.

We were rich and that was all that mattered right then. Maisie had achieved what she had wanted, if we kept to the plan Trevor would never get his hands on the diamonds. And neither would Hughes.

"We've only gone and done it, Cy. Maisie would be so proud."

"We need to get these back inside to that jeweller. He can swap them for real money for us." Cy was beside himself.

"We can come back later and get the others as well," I added, seeing the beauty in Maisie's, or Kim's, plan. "As far as Hughes and anyone else knows, the other stash doesn't exist. And even if Hughes finds out about these, he'll think that's all there was."

Clever Maisie! Clever Kim! Not forgetting clever me!

"How are we going to get these past Trevor and Hughes, not to mention the police?" Cy asked. "Knowing you, I expect you've got an idea."

"I have but one of us will have to go outside again."

To my surprise, Cy volunteered. "I'll do it," he said almost immediately, "whatever it is."

When he heard my plan he laughed. "That's a brilliant idea." He put the suit helmet back on and I checked his seals. He took everything but the bag of diamonds and strode confidently into the airlock. The door shut behind him as I got out of my suit and sat in the driver's seat. I watched while he did what I had suggested.

It only took him a couple of minutes, when the inner door opened and he took off the helmet, his eyes shone with joy. "I did it!" he said. "Now we just need to make sure we don't get them mixed up."

"I'm going to Hecate now," I said as he hung up his suit and took his seat. He nodded, looking more sombre as I drove out of the canyon and turned back towards the spot where they had found Maisie. I didn't need the map, the position was burned in my mind.

"This trip has changed a lot of things," he muttered.

"What do you mean?"

"We came here because we thought it was suicide. Now we know it wasn't and we've got the reason for it all. And we've got a pretty good idea who did it. Once we've got shot of the diamonds, we can go to Mayer and tell him about the video."

We arrived at Hecate. I stopped and we sat in silence for a few minutes, there was a minor dust devil swirling around the cliffs and the red dust blew over us. We took out the bottle, ate our lunch and toasted Maisie, until control called us again.

There was no need to put it off any longer. It was time to get back inside and finish things up. The shuttle would be leaving for the station in a few days and we could be on it.

I started the Rover up and swung it towards the airlock. As I approached it, I could see that the light was green. It was open this end. I called for permission to enter.

"Hold, OLC rig," said Control, "we have one outward movement booked."

I stopped; we were about five hundred metres from the airlock. The green light went out and a red one winked on. The door slid shut.

"What's that?" asked Cy.

"Don't worry, there's a rig coming out, then we can go in."

"OK," he replied, "nothing to get excited about then?"

"No, it's normal, the outward rig will have a booked slot, like we did."

We sat for a moment, then the radio crackled.

"Control, this is Douglas Trading, we're out for a familiarisation trip towards Hensens Ridge. Licence ID Jordan 429 three POB."

Cy sat upright, "That's them."

"And they're heading out, so they won't be waiting for us inside." I finished off the thought.

"We're sorted then, they must be off to try and find the stuff."

Feeling relieved we watched as the outer door opened. Permission was granted and the familiar black Rover came out and turned towards the ridge.

"OLC rig, you can enter."

We drove into the airlock and reported. The door shut behind us and the numbers started to increase on the board. Then my phone rang.

Chapter 34

"Who's that?" asked Cy.

"Unknown number," I said as I answered it.

"Hello, Andi." It was Trevor, of all the times to call me.

"Oh hi, Trevor, I haven't heard from you for a while, you OK?"

"I'm fine, you shopping somewhere?"

"Yeah, I'll meet you later for a coffee?"

His tone changed. "Alright, Andi, it's over. When you get out of the airlock, drive into the service area and you'd better have the stuff." The call ended.

"What did he want?" Cy asked.

"He knows." I was shaking. "He said I had to drive into the service area."

"What?"

The number reached fifty per cent.

"Don't ask me how."

Sixty-five per cent.

"I'm out of here. I'll try and get the cavalry," Cy said and opened the door. There was a hiss as we lost some atmosphere, the airlock was only at ninety per cent; any less and the Rover's door wouldn't have opened. I thought the operator was going to shout on the radio but the control room was on the other side to the door. Cy dropped into the airlock and went to the side door, the one the lockmaster had used when we visited. He got through it before the steel inner door opened. I pulled the Rover's outer door shut behind him and drove out, slowly.

Ahead was the slip road, straight on was back to the city, the way was blocked by a team of workmen. They were probably the suits that Shev had seen digging in the care home, making sure I did what I was told. Without a choice, I went into the service area.

When the tunnel opened out, there was one other vehicle in sight. An interior buggy. Trevor was sat inside it; he waved so I parked up and got out.

Bugger! In the excitement I still had the two bags, one in each pocket. I should have hidden them in the Rover, but there wasn't time now. I was back inside and in full dozy mode. So much for the plan. Cy should have been on his way to Kevic by now. Trevor's call had messed it all up, things had gone hopelessly wrong.

"Hi, Trevor," I said. "How…?"

"Did you get them?" he asked me, straight out.

"Get what? I've just been out to Hensens Ridge, it's beautiful."

"Don't piss me about, Andi; you wouldn't use this airlock to go there, or an OLC Rover. You've been out and got the diamonds haven't you? And where's Cy?"

So it was out in the open. "Is that what Maisie told you was out there?"

He laughed. "No, she wouldn't tell me squat. Hughes told me the whole story."

"And how did you know I'd gone out there?"

"Lesleigh from the hire company told me you'd asked about renting a vehicle, I just had to follow the tracker. Where is he? He's here somewhere, you said two POB when you left, where's the rest of your double act?"

I was fuming. Lesleigh, the girl from the hire shop. Lesleigh with the long blonde hair. It made sense. "Is she your new squeeze then, Trevor?" He had the grace to look embarrassed.

"What can I say, she wasn't on the scene until after," he said. I didn't believe him.

"I saw her hair, in your apartment. Is she in on this as well?"

"Not in that way, she's been over to mine a couple of times; but she doesn't know about the diamonds. I asked her to tell me if you hired a Rover. She just thinks I'm going to be paying the bill for you."

Now was probably not the best time to tell him that 'mine' wasn't, or at least, wouldn't be for much longer.

"But I didn't rent a Rover from her."

"Hughes screwed up when he let you go, we didn't know where you'd got to. Then we realised that all we could do was keep an eye on the airlocks." He grinned. "Remember the swipe card you took from the apartment?"

I did. "Yes."

"Well it's got a chip in it; every time you use an airlock it's recorded. Lesleigh just had to monitor the logs."

Oh crap! "So you knew I went out before the storm?"

"Yep! In the OLC Rover as well! That was smart. I guess they're your friends from the station, we know you've been in touch."

Smooth smug git. "She'll soon be off, you know; Lesleigh, when she finds out what an arsehole you really are."

"You loved me once." Ouch!

"Until you showed me your true colours, Trevor. It was pretty low, getting into Maisie's pants by making out that we were over."

He smiled at the memory. "Happy days, or at least it was until the bucket hit me on the head."

"It was all a lie wasn't it? The whole story to get me to come here."

"You're too clever for your own good. I needed you here to get the message from Maisie and to work it all out, she wouldn't bloody tell me."

"So you killed her?"

"Of course not." He sounded hurt; for a moment I desperately wanted to believe him.

"I didn't want her to die. I fed her the sleeping pills to make sure that Hughes couldn't get her to take him out. I didn't want to but I couldn't see any other way. She wouldn't tell me, I thought I had no choice, I thought I would save her. But the pills took too long to work."

Could that be true, could Trevor have been trying to protect her, or was it just another lie?

"I borrowed money from the wrong men, they said that I had to help them find the stuff; they had heard that the stones were on Mars and that someone in the home where Maisie worked knew where they were. They wanted me to get her to find out. I asked her and she said I was crazy and stupid. She wouldn't help me. I knew they would kill me if I didn't go along. I had to tell her the whole story, about the money and everything. That was it; she was going to leave me."

"I don't blame her."

"Then Hughes turned up and threatened her; the gang had worked it out. They didn't set out to kill her, I fed her the sleeping pills, like I said, I hadn't realised how long they would take to work. She had time to get out, she must have fallen asleep on her way. Hughes didn't go out, he was frightened to go. He had his men outside; they were going to follow her and get the diamonds. They said that she had suddenly stopped on the way. They were fed up with her messing them about, so they just left her by the rocks, made it look like suicide."

"Why didn't you stop her going? Slow her down, give the pills time to work?"

"I couldn't, Hughes and his boys made her go. Even though I knew what would happen. I knew she was drugged, I couldn't let on. Hughes would have killed me for messing him around. As it was he went mad when the men came back and told him what they had done. 'How am I going to get the stones now?' he said. He thumped one of them and I thought that he was going to shoot me. Then I wondered; maybe she had told you, perhaps if I could get you here you could work it out."

"God, Trevor, you're even more of a shit than I thought you were, you might not have killed her but you let her die to save your own stupid neck."

"You shouldn't talk to me like that, Andi, I've got the gun." He pulled it out of his pocket. The barrel caught in the material and he looked away from me while he untangled it. I was going to run but before I could, he got himself sorted out.

He pointed it at me. "And I was right in the end; you came here, worked it out and got me the stones. I'm alive and when I've paid Hughes what I owe him I'll be rich. We still make a great team; we really should get back together."

It was so preposterous that I almost laughed.

"Get stuffed, Trevor! The only reason you wanted me here was to work it out and find the stones for you. You never cared about our friendship."

"I knew she'd leave you clues. Hughes agreed to get you and finance your stay, he's around somewhere. They blocked the road with a fake repair squad. We were waiting for you to come back in with the diamonds."

"Do you know how much the stones I have here are worth? Do you even know that most of it was out of date banknotes, there were only a few diamonds?"

"No, and I couldn't care less if it's unicorn shit. All I know is that it's enough to pay off my debts and leave enough to set me up."

"Do you really think that Hughes is going to let you keep any of it?"

"Of course he will, we have a deal. Hand 'em over."

The gun was pointed at me, this was it, where was my backup? I was in urgent need of a knight on a white charger; Mayner and his merry men should have turned up by now. Failing that, Cy would do, just as long as he got me out of here pronto! And where the hell had he got to?

~~~~

Cy appeared from behind the Rover, he might have been there listening for a while for all I knew. I hope he had because it would have made him very angry.

"I've fixed everything, Andi." He looked at Trevor; saw the gun in his hand. "What's going on," he shouted. Trevor turned and raised the gun, pointing it at him.

"Look out, Cy!" I shouted.

"Go on then," said Cy, advancing. "You haven't got the balls to shoot me." Was he crazy? I know he'd said that he wanted Trevor where he couldn't run but this was ridiculous.

"Stop right there," said Trevor. "I'll do it." The gun wavered in his hands. Did it drop a fraction?

Cy never stopped. "Come on then," he taunted him. "You always reckoned you were a better man than me, prove it, do it."

He launched himself at Trevor who backed off a pace and swung the gun back up. Surely he would fire? Cy was too quick, in a blur of movement he grabbed Trevor's gun arm and they wrestled. The gun clattered to the floor and they danced over it. Cy was bigger and stronger but Trevor was smart, he used Cy's weight against him and tripped him. Cy hit his head on the cave wall and fell, his face bloody. The collision had been hard; Cy was unconscious, was he dead? If Trevor had killed him he would have me to contend with, even more than he did already.

I had been backing away, creeping closer to the door of the Rover while all this was going on, I don't know what my plan was, the bullets would have gone through the windscreen of the Rover and that would have stopped me. But there were heavy things in the Rover, I could use them as weapons. I never made it.

"Stop, Andi," Trevor shouted. He was a different Trevor now. He walked calmly toward the gun and picked it up. It was covered in dust, if I had been quicker I could have grabbed it instead of trying to get into the Rover but it was too late for that now. The question was, would I have the guts to walk towards Trevor like that? He hadn't shot at Cy and surely I meant more to him than he did.

He faced me. I thought that I could see right down the barrel of the gun, it looked like a tunnel.

"You won't use it on me, will you?" I said confidently.

His answer was to shoot at my feet; I jumped as the bullet whined away.

Bloody hell, what did that say? That he was less concerned with shooting me than he was with shooting Cy? And I had thought he was the love of my life.

"You've changed, Trevor," I said. "How come you didn't shoot at Cy?"

He didn't answer, the gun wavered and I was just debating doing something pointless and futile like rushing him when he finally spoke.

He shrugged. "I had to do what they wanted. I'm sorry for the way things turned out. Of course I am. I never wanted Maisie to get involved. I honestly thought that I was doing the right thing drugging her. I really thought it would keep her out of the way. Now give me the bag."

Was that true or just weasel words from a man running out of options? I tried to remember which bag was in which pocket.

"Last chance," he said.

I pulled the bag from my left pocket and tossed it over to him. I think it was the one he was supposed to have. "Here you are then."

He caught it. "Is that all?" he said. "Hughes said there would be a lot more than that."

"It's all there was. Why don't you go out and have a look yourself?"

Hughes came into view. He was dressed in overalls; he must have been out there blocking the road. Trevor saw him and relaxed.

"Have you got it?" said Hughes.

"Yes," said Trevor, as he held up the bag.

Chapter 35

Hughes pulled a pistol from his belt and shot him, casually and without breaking stride.

Trevor stepped back and fell to his knees, a look of surprise on his face. He coughed and blood spurted. Without another sound he collapsed and lay still. The bag fell to the floor. Hughes stooped and picked it up; he felt the texture of the bag's contents under the cloth. His eyes took in me and Cy; he looked at his still body and bloodied face and my panic.

"I've wanted to do that for ages," he said. "He was pissing me right off, how'd you ever live with him?"

There was no answer to that. So much for their deal. I just shrugged.

"I ought to shoot you now," he said. "But I should really thank you first."

Another two men appeared and joined Hughes. "What have you done?" the older one said, looking at Trevor lying in a pool of blood, Cy in a heap with his face covered in the red stuff.

"He was no longer essential," said Hughes. "Now it's these two's turn."

"Have you got the stones?" Hughes lifted the bag, the two shrugged and turned away. "Looks like you've redeemed yourself," said the older one.

"Whatever you need to do then," added the other.

Hughes looked relieved. "Sorry," he said to me.

"Let me guess; it's not personal."

He nodded. "It was never personal, get over there, by your friend."

I moved over to Cy, knelt and held his hand, feeling for the pulse in his wrist. He stirred and his eyes fluttered open.

"Where am I?" he said, shaking his head and trying to sit up. Oh joy, he was alive, but for how long? Perhaps he would have been better asleep and never waking. Like poor Maisie. Just in that moment, when I knew I was going to die, I envied her painless death.

"Goodbye," said Hughes. Something flew through the air and landed by his feet, a small grey sphere. He looked down at it as it went pop. He moved to kick it away, but as he lifted his foot he toppled over and lay still.

There were more pops. His mates turned and crumpled to the ground. "Gas," I said to Cy, as one of the spheres landed by us. It popped. "I told you; the cavalry…"

Chapter 36

I woke up to find a policeman standing over me. I was still by the airlock so I can't have been out for very long. I turned my head and felt sick. Hughes and his buddies were in handcuffs and were being loaded into a police Rover. Cy was receiving attention from a paramedic and where Trevor had fallen there was a bloodstained patch of earth. A shrouded figure lay on a trolley nearby. Trevor had got in well over his head and paid the price.

"Is she awake?" said a voice out of my sight, it was Detective Mayner; the uniform turned.

"She's just waking up," he said. Mayner came into sight as I lifted my head up as far as I could without wanting to barf.

"How are you feeling, Ms Pett?" he asked me. "Are you in any pain?"

I did a quick check, wiggled my toes and fingers and shuffled my bum. Nope, it all seemed to be functioning and I couldn't feel any part complaining. I had been right; the police were still following Hughes and keeping an eye on me. They had come to my, our, rescue. Not soon enough to save Trevor though.

"I'm OK, I think," I said and tried to get up. Whoa, it was like when you wake up after a party, feel fine and then you move and everything starts spinning.

"Take it easy," the policeman said. "The gas takes a while to clear through your system."

I lay back down, feeling the bag press into my right side as my jacket fell open under me. Good; it was still there and no-one was the wiser, better try and keep it that way.

I could hear Cy waking up. Turning to him, I saw that the medic had cleaned a lot of the blood from Cy's head and he looked far more presentable than he had done. He was sitting up, hopefully his brain wouldn't have been too scrambled and he would stick to the story. He grinned at me and patted his side pocket. I winked.

"You seem to have solved a mystery," Mayner said, he was holding the bag that Hughes had taken from Trevor's dead hand. "It's strange that such a small bag could be the cause of so much grief." He opened it and I held my breath. It would have been just like me to have thrown him the wrong one.

He started to laugh. "Look," he said, tipping it upside down, the red pebbles and earth that I had got Cy to put in the bag before we came back cascaded onto the ground. I joined in, although my laugh was more of relief than anything else.

"So it was all a myth, after all these years," he said between chuckles. "Someone must have found them and removed the diamonds ages ago."

All the policemen and medics were laughing; hopefully we wouldn't be searched before we could get back into town and see the jeweller. That was what I had wanted Trevor to think. If I had to I was going to let him have the bag of pebbles and then he might just react like Mayner had. Leaving us in the clear.

"You know," Mayner said, "I wasn't sure about you, Ms Pett. You're not as daft as you would like people to believe. I was pretty sure you knew what you were doing but I thought that right now I'd be arresting you for handling stolen property, wasting police time and all sorts of other things." He paused and I waited. "But things don't always work out like you expect and as all you had was a bag of rocks I can hardly make that stick, can I?"

"No, I guess not," I answered, trying to avoid any sort of expression.

He looked at me again. "And anyway, I suppose I should thank you for helping us reduce the gang problem a little, we'll get you to the hospital, get you checked out, then I reckon you'll be leaving us on the next shuttle." The last bit was said as an instruction, not a comment; I got the message.

"We have a few people to see first, take the Rover back, say thank you and that sort of thing, but yes, we'll be off as soon as we can."

It was a pity that all the police had was a bag of pebbles but maybe now they and everyone would think that the whole idea that the missing diamonds were on Mars really was just a myth. We had a bag of stones for Kevic, they would give him something to do for a while, it meant that we had made a profit on the trip. And once the fuss had died down, we could come back and pick the rest up any time we wanted. Nobody knew about the second bag, just as I had hoped.

In the meantime, I wanted to get back to the station and see everyone again, especially Derek and Maz. I expect Cy wanted to see Greg as well.

"I can't wait to get back and have a rest," I said to Cy. "I told you the police would turn up and save us."

He smiled. "They cut it a bit fine but they did. I like the going home idea. Do you think we could have a few quiet months now, please?"

The end, for now.

Andorra Pett will return soon, here's the start of the next adventure, *Andorra Pett and her Sister.*

"When a sister hates you, then that really is the end of the world."

Chapter 1

The fluorescent tubes flickered in their yellowed plastic fittings; the air was rich with the smells of stale alcohol and unwashed humanity. It was as unfamiliar to the lady stood in front of the desk as the surface of the moon.

"You can have one phone call," said the uniformed man on the other side of the desk. Three stripes on his sleeve would make him a sergeant, she idly thought. Behind her, people sat sprawled, drunk and bloodied, the result of another busy Friday night in Greenwich. She had avoided all eye contact, if she didn't look, then they weren't here and neither was she.

More uniforms bustled around her, the room was filled with conversation. She shifted from foot to foot, her soles sticking to whatever it was that adorned the worn plastic tiles. She didn't really want to speculate on its origins.

The uniform was still talking. "Before we record your possessions and take you to the cells, do you understand the charges against you and your rights?"

'Oh God!' she thought, it sounded so final and such a surprise. When the doorbell had rung, only a few short hours ago, the last thing she had been expecting was the policemen and the detectives who had swarmed over her house and garden. Cupboards had been emptied and holes were dug in the immaculate turf. Muddy boots trampled over the shag pile. Dogs panted and strained to sniff in all the corners. Her computer was disconnected and placed in a box, together with all the papers from her business. It felt like an invasion, yet all her pleas for an explanation were met with silence. In the eyes of the searchers, she could see contempt and the world-weary presumption of guilt. In desperation she had faced one of the uniformed men and shouted into his face, "What are you doing in my house, what do you think I've done?"

Again, there was no answer. She grabbed the man, wanting to shake a response from him. Instantly she was spun around, her arms were forced behind her back and handcuffs were snapped in place, digging into her wrists.

"Don't make it worse," the policeman hissed in her ear, his breath hot on her neck. "You'll add assault to the list if you're not careful." She forced herself to calm down, rage would get her nowhere.

The charges against her were read out as she was cautioned by one of the detectives; they were the second stage of the nightmare. Until a week ago, she wouldn't have had a clue how they fitted into her life. All she did was run a modest shop, selling ethnic goods, cane furniture, ceramics and hand-woven fabric cushions. It was *Fairtrade* for goodness' sake!

She listened in disbelief as they charged her with receiving controlled substances and laundering the proceeds of criminal activity. But she had to accept that the accusations were, on the face of it at least, correct. The way she had found out had been just as bad. But she was saving that for the statement she knew she would have to make, sooner or later, so she had said nothing. And now she was here.

The nightmare had all started a few days ago. She was unpacking a delivery when she knocked over a vase that she was putting on display in the shop. There had been a few small plastic bags of something white taped together inside it, they were mixed in with the broken shards and her heart lurched when she saw them. Stupidly, as it now turned out, instead of calling the police, she had panicked and thrown everything away, double wrapped in black bags, trying to pretend that she had never seen them.

"Who do you want us to call?" the police sergeant repeated. "Husband, partner, parents, solicitor?"

As he suggested each, she thought, 'No, I haven't got any of them,' and if she was honest, even some of her so-called friends would not want to be associated with her now. At this time of day, they probably wouldn't answer or be too smashed or stoned to be of much use to her anyway. In their world of dinner parties and liberal values, they all professed to despise the police and authority in general as instruments of the overbearing state, they would avoid being seen in such a place as a police station voluntarily if they possibly could.

There was only one person who could help her sort this mess out and she still hesitated, even though she had to call. To say that they had had their differences over the years would not be an exaggeration. She was sure that they would come through, now that it really mattered. Because when the chips were down, that was what you did.

"Call my sister," she said. "I'll get you the number." She fished around in the bag laid on the counter.

The policeman looked mystified. "Your sister? It's up to you entirely but most people ask for their solicitor. You are aware just how serious all this is?"

"That's fine," she answered, still desperately hoping that it was all a fuss over nothing; that in the end common sense would prevail. "Just get her; she'll know what to do."

She passed him the card that had been in her purse so long that it was rubbed and scuffed by all the coins it had pressed against. He took it and peered at the writing.

"Is this some sort of a joke?" he asked in a puzzled tone. "AC Couture, a clothes shop in Greenwich? It's been closed for at least a year. And Andorra Pett, *the* Andorra Pett? That's your sister?"

The woman nodded. "Just use the mobile number; it should still be the same. Tell her that her sister Argentia's in deep trouble and she should get here as quickly as she can."

The sergeant shrugged his shoulders. "OK then, if it's what you want." Peering at the card he dialled the number.

"It's ringing."

Andorra Pett and her Sister will be published in 2019

I hope that you have enjoyed this book.

If you've enjoyed reading this story, please would you consider leaving a review on the website where you purchased it. Even if it's only a few words, it will be appreciated and might just help someone else discover their next great read!
   Thank you very much.
   Richard.
   www.richarddeescifi.co.uk

www.ingramcontent.com/pod-product-compliance
Ingram Content Group UK Ltd.
Pitfield, Milton Keynes, MK11 3LW, UK
UKHW041414180426
11947UKWH00007B/120